D1520644

33 boroughs shorts EAST

ENFIELD
WALTHAM FOREST
REDBRIDGE
HAVERING
HACKNEY
BARKING & DAGENHAM
TOWER HAMLETS
NEWHAM
SOUTHWARK
GREENWICH
BEXLEY
LEWISHAM
BROMLEY

Contents

HAVERING

Ultimate Satisfaction Everyday

Ultimate Satisfaction Everyday

Susannah Rickards

Greg Mason was a loser. He flogged dry dog food door to door round the outskirts of Romford and would have cocked up even this career had he not married the boss's daughter, Eileen, because one unusual night he felt able to ask for her hand. Her father, glad to be shot of the sniping little mare, rewarded Greg with a sales franchise in Emerson Park, an easy, salubrious territory that earned him the resentment of fellow salesmen. But after her father retired, Eileen barged in on the business with a thirst for wealth that Greg found unseemly. She booked herself onto deal-closing seminars and then exploited her new-found knowledge, hogging the phone when orders came in, pushing protein enriched treats that Greg was sure played havoc with dogs' kidneys. She upped the price each time new stock arrived. When business dwindled she blamed him. One sub-zero night she locked him out of the house in a game that soon turned humourless. To drum initiative into him, she said. But he gave up and went off to kip on a banquette in The Mariners, handing two months' Peak Fitness Doberman rations to the barman by way of thanks. For Eileen, that was the end.

Greg's solicitor lost him custody of the kids. He saw them twice a month, in charred playparks and cinemas. They spotted food on his tie and traded Yu-Gi-Oh cards with each other under burger-bar tables, ignoring his questions. When they parted his eldest said, 'Laters,' and wouldn't return his hug.

One afternoon he was delivering to a leafy detached on Woodlands Avenue when Eileen's car pulled up at the mansion next door and Greg's kids tumbled out. That unscheduled glimpse of their uncombed heads and restless limbs kicked his heart. He was gearing up to greet them when through the hedge he spied a man younger than himself belting a ball in the air and saw the blue curve of a swimming pool. Still, they were his kids so he called to them. Their footsteps stopped and he heard his youngest whisper, 'Dog alert. Hurry. Or he'll want to talk to us.' The gate clanged as they headed for the pool.

Greg drove away, not back to his rented room above a shop on the Hornchurch Road but down to the Thames at Rainham, his childhood stomping ground. He parked where the road ran out at the entrance to the municipal tip. They'd grassed over the mountains of landfill since he'd last visited. A smell of toasting rice from the Tilda processing plant dominated the air. On either side of the water, factory chimneys steamed and machinery whirred, softer than the birdsong from the Purfleet sanctuary a mile away, as if industry itself ticked by unmanned. No need of human interference. No need for men like him.

Downriver some wag had placed a skeleton frame of a diver out in the water, as if caught to his waist in the mud. He bet the council had commissioned it. They had ever-wilier ruses for squandering Greg's tax. Some self-appointed Thames Gateway Artist-in-River-Residence probably landed himself a fat grant for cobbling together found objects from the council tip or shoreline rubbish, and called it sculpture. But though he wanted to berate it, he found himself drawn to the diver, and stood a while, watching the tidal water run through the mesh of his torso, swilling about in the empty cage where his heart and guts should be. The late afternoon light on the wide river, the sounds of the birds and machines and the tide all filled his head and distilled his thoughts to this:

He sought one thing. One thing he was proud to have done in his life.

He'd lived all his life in Havering, this sleepy rural second cousin of a London borough, and that placidity seemed bred inside his bones.

At Hi-Pro motivational conferences he'd met salesmen who'd moved out from Bow and the Isle of Dogs. Living here was a sign of making good. There was an edge to them, a pride born of having escaped the city. And there were the ones who'd moved in from outlying Essex villages, hungry for all those Romford doorsteps, every one a sale in the making. But Greg was not edgy, not hungry. Until now, Havering had suited him. He'd been quiet and kind and satisfied all through his life, but that was from disposition not choice. Should he have fought for Eileen? Would a bitter custody battle have shown his boys a depth or quality of love they doubted now? He tried to remember how he'd filled his time before she'd commandeered it. Hours at the run-down gym in the outhouse of The Admiralty, weight-lifting. He'd been strong back then, in body. Perhaps that's what Eileen had liked. Perhaps she'd imagined that strength ran through him. Why, he'd been so physically powerful as a single man that once he'd lifted a car to free a child trapped beneath.

Greg breathed in, stepped forward towards the river. At his feet a thousand washed up water bottles and coffee cups looked up at him like a stadium crowd. A sudden calm infused him. That was the One Thing. He had forgotten it until now but he had saved a life.

Back then his energy outstripped his patience for exercise. He'd done two circuits that night, all his usual weights upped by ten, and not felt tired. The other gym-jocks invited him for a pint and he turned them down, not wanting to blunt the fizzing health he felt. It was November, early dark. He crossed the yard onto the steep main road. Outside Costcutter's a car pulled up and Kerry, Dean Fletcher's girlfriend, got out. Her knew her by sight. Prettiness masked by acne, wet look curls, long legs.

He watched casually, his eye drawn simply because hers was the only movement on the street. The spill of light from Costcutter's window framed her, adding potency to her ordinary actions, as if she were in a film. Kerry went to the boot to fetch something. As she did, the rear door opened, her little girl scrambled out and toddled in front of the car. Greg was about to call out for Kerry to watch for her when he realised the car was rolling downhill. It nudged the child and she fell in its path. The car's front wheel rolled onto her hair and her trailing fur hood, trapping her, inching towards her soft wide face. All this in seconds as he sprinted towards them. Kerry screamed into the night: 'Oh someone – Oh God!'

Greg reached them, squatted, lifted the car clear, not aware of its weight, just the hot strength flooding through him. Kerry pulled her child free, face buried against her saying, 'Ashley, bubba, wake up, talk to mumma.'

He released the car and it seemed light, bouncing as it landed. When he stood, it felt like he kept on rising and rising until the world were navel height to him and he could run his hands over its surface to make it right. Now other people, scenting crisis, joined them: the checkout man from Costcutter, waving a lollipop at Ashley, an old woman quoting out-of-hours doctors' numbers by heart. The cashier pushed the lollipop against Ashley's lips. Her eyes opened, blank, staring past her mother to the sky, then she opened her mouth and shuddered. Her scalp was bald in patches, and bleeding, but the checkout man said scalps do bleed a lot, his brother's did when he got attacked, and it looks worse than it is, see her neck's moving and she's breathing. Kerry kept thanking him for the lollipop. She didn't thank Greg. She moved away from the car into a dim side street, the pensioner at her shoulder, advising.

For a moment the cashier looked like he might ask Greg something, but some teenagers started shouting in his shop and he went after them. Greg stood alone in the street with Dean's car. The power that had brooded inside him was gone. He felt clean and his skin stung, like after a day in the sea and sun. That night he asked Eileen to marry him. Weeks later, her dad set him up with the new franchise and they moved to Upminster. He hadn't seen Kerry or the child since.

***

How had he not carried that with him over the years? He wasn't sure he'd even told his children. He and his wife weren't given to reminiscing and the boys were not the curious kind. He must have told Eileen the night he proposed. As he stood looking out across the wide river, he thought perhaps he had and that she'd slid her cool hands over his biceps, bringing his mind back to her, where she believed it should be.

He turned to head back. Along the Thames, beside the Tilda loading jetty, the fleet of dumped concrete barges had shifted over the years. They stood half-submerged now in the river sand, hulls pointing at the sky. In childhood he had imagined the barges solid and wondered how a boat made of concrete could float. Now that they were disintegrating, he saw it: their skins were paper thin, their frames no sturdier than the diver's mesh. His father used to walk him here some Sundays, pointing out the council plaque that said the barges had formed part of the Mulberry Harbour, played their part in winning the war. He'd heard that disputed in recent years, as though the barges had fancied themselves in their youth and now their crumbling frames shed doubt on previous honours.

Seventeen years ago he'd lifted her free. He got into his car and headed back along the service road from the tip towards Rainham. Ahead of him the A13 ran on stilts over the salt marshes, feeding traffic into London and out to the ferry ports. He scanned the cars for green 'L' plates. Ashley could be gunning along nicely on that road overhead right now, her head full of a trip to Paris or a West End show.

The image pleased him. Over the following days he developed it, gave her a new dress on the back seat of the car, various occasions for wearing it. Not for Ashley a life standing on the footbridge, fending off the slipstream of the Eurostar as it hurtled through Rainham station. She'd be inside the train, a glossy mag open between her pretty hands. She'd escaped death. She'd not be one to let life grow over her like weeds.

His own boys remained morose, uncouth, as Ashley, the daughter he'd never had but now laid claim to, blossomed. He was there at her graduation when she tossed her mortarboard into the air where it freeze-framed. She smiled delightedly when he, not a patient, walked into her surgery. But why stop there? 'Hey Greg,' she breathed into the mike from the stage at O2. 'This song's for you.'

The Fletchers lived three floors up on a council run in Harold Hill. It had taken Greg eight days to find them. He'd contacted many Fletchers in the old neighbourhood, a sack of Hi-Pro Dog at the ready, as an excuse. At this door he got a feeling, a settling round his shoulders. This was where a sympathetic Kerry, an ever-grateful Dean would introduce him like a lost relative: This is Greg. He saved your life when you were small. He'd like to meet you now if that's OK.

A middle-aged woman opened the door. It took him a moment to realise she was Kerry. Her drenched curls had been replaced by a helmet of purple hair, and the acne had given way to smoker's lines.

'Kerry. It's Greg Mason, remember me?'

'Might.'

'I wanted to see Ashley.'

'Ash,' Kerry called through the flat, 'Got call.' No welcome, no sign of surprise, but she stood aside and let him pass into her orange lounge which housed a cabinet, a sofa spewing foam and a tin dog-bowl.

Kerry turned on him, fingers flicking unseen fluff from her sleeves. 'You sort her meds before you're out that door, all right? She's back forty-eight hours and already she's doing my nut. And I want her housed cos she ain't staying here. Got that? This is my home and she's–'

A girl came into the lounge. She had her mother's dark curls. On each cheek was a weeping sore, like a second set of eyes, larger and brighter than the small dull ones above them. She went to the sofa and lay on it, pulling her jeans down low on her hips to reveal a hard ball of a belly which she kneaded, groaning and twisting.

Greg stood feeling cumbersome, searching for the right comment. He landed on a genial and soothing, 'The midwife's on her way, is she?'

'Can you stand in the doorway, where you ain't in the way,' Kerry said. 'She ain't in labour, she's coming off methadone. Ain't you even read her file?'

'Sorry,' said Greg. She must think he was a medical man or from social services. Her misunderstanding pleased him, showed she saw in him a man who helped others, changed lives. He wanted to be that man and turned to watch Ashley with what he hoped passed for tender, professional assessment.

Ashley yanked at her jeans, trying to undo the waistband, then gave up and her hands went limp.

'It's freezing in here,' she said.

'It's up full whack, Ash,' Kerry replied.

'Oh, I'm not gonna make it!'

Ashley rushed from the room, bent double.

Kerry studied him. 'You're new, ain't you? What was you before?'

'Sales,' he said. 'Pet foods.'

'Hah!' Kerry squealed.

She retrieved a key from her sweater, unlocked the cabinet and took out a bottle of liqueur. It had a stick of sugar running through it, shaped like coral. When she'd poured two shots she locked the cabinet and tucked the key back into her bra. 'Not a good game this, is it? Need a bit of this and that to see us through. Suck it up.' She handed one to him – a challenge. He knocked it back. Like candied fire. It was years since he'd drunk anything but beer.

From the bathroom Ashley retched and moaned and flushed.

'Ain't you got questions?' Kerry asked.

'Would she like to be readmitted?'

'What? To Holloway?' Kerry screeched a laugh, caught his confused eye, screeched again. 'Dunno, pet shop boy, shall we ask her?'

'I meant hospital. What's she on?'

'Nothing. Lost your notes? They cancelled the meth script soon as she got out. Don't give her nothing to tide her over, cos she'd only flog it. She got to go up the GP but she won't.'

Ashley came back into the room. Her jeans zip was undone to ease her bloated belly. She looked up at him with both sets of eyes, then her head drooped and she shivered.

'Hey,' said Greg. He took off his jacket to give to her.

'Oi, she's burning up. You got to keep cool, Ash. You only think you're freezing. Open the window, Keyworker.'

Greg opened the door to the balcony, onto bland, summer air. The estate spread out beneath him, its chalk and smoke buildings, the broccoli trees of Duck Wood to the East, and traffic snaking south towards Romford centre with its glass land of shops and bars. It wasn't that bad a place. It didn't deserve such helpless attitudes from him or Ash or Kerry. In the late afternoon light it looked full of possibilities.

'Hey Ashley, come and stand out here,' he said.

'I got the heebies.'

'Well … have them out here in the sun.'

'Bloody hell.'

But she stumbled out towards him, still grinding her fists into the swollen rock of her belly. He gripped her arm. Her body was surprisingly compliant; it fell against his. He righted her, trying to steer her round so he could stare into her eyes but she wouldn't meet his gaze. She kept squirming and keening about her bellyache, like a spoilt child. The diplomas and silk dresses and concerts, even her ruddy driving license detached themselves from her and sailed from the balcony, sailed down like the clothes of a spurned husband. All his plans for her, all she might have been, dispatched towards the blue van up on bricks in the yard below, from which music with a brain-stopping beat thumped back at him.

'Look around you!' he said. 'I gave this to you.'

'Eh? What?'

'Look!' He shook her gently. Paternally, he thought, but she wailed. The pillowslips drying on the balcony opposite, the music from the knock-off motor below, even these should seem marvellous to her.

'Get off me. I'm dizzy.'

'Oi!' Kerry came to the balcony doorway. Greg let Ashley go and she crawled inside to the settee. Kerry beckoned Greg in but blocked his way so he had to squeeze past her.

'Reckons Social recruited him off a bloody pet shop, Ash,' she said. 'Mind your step or he'll kennel you.' Up close she smelled of sweat and bleach. The skin under her eyes and at her chin hung in frail loops. Greg had to fight the impulse to tuck a finger up under the flaps, as he did with dogs whose faces hung that way.

'You ain't her keyworker. What are you?'

'Greg Mason,' he said. 'Dean's mate from school, remember? The car outside Costcutter. Ashley fell under the wheel. I lifted the car.'

'What?'

'I lifted the car so you could pull her free.'

Kerry's eyes flickered. 'I ain't saying you're lying,' she said, 'but I don't recall. She was a terror. We was in and out Queens' A & E so much they almost give us her own bed. Ash, remember that time you was running on top that Spitfire at Hornchurch aerodrome and you fell and that squaddie what caught you split his arm up, breaking your fall?'

'Nuh,' said Ashley.

'You was only small.'

Now she'd begun, Kerry went on describing all the others like him, leaping to preserve Ashley's treasurable life. Pig-thick of him to imagine his action had made him unique.

As Ashley rocked, a bull terrier appeared from behind the settee and trotted to the empty bowl. It yapped at Kerry.

'Tough,' she told it. 'Ain't got none. You'll have to wait.'

Greg walked past them into the hall. The sack of dog biscuits he'd brought as an excuse to call was still by the front door. He carried it through. Kerry was on the sofa now, embracing Ashley, and the terrier was up on the cushions with them, snouting at Ashley's hair.

Greg opened the bag and shook some biscuits free. The dog jumped on them, the choppy exertions of his tail a frantic mimic of Ashley's rocking.

'What you'll find,' said Greg, 'is that this is comprehensive life assurance for your pet in pellet form. Health. Vitality. Balance. Ultimate satisfaction everyday.'

The words came easily. He explained how the simple daily discipline of selecting this food form over the bewildering array of inferior choices available in today's supermarkets would enable them as owners to get the most from their dog and would benefit their pet throughout his days. His spiel had never run so smoothly. When he'd finished Greg set the sack beside the door, and though they had their backs to him he bowed. Coming back up to standing, his body felt solid, as though he inhabited it once again, after a long period of it standing vacant. He'd found her. He'd provided this small service. He could leave now and he'd be OK.

BARKING & DAGENHAM
Unfinished Business

Unfinished Business

Martin Machado

'I, Mary Geraldine Sumpter, being of sound mind, request Mr Hertzberg – or whoever replaces him in the event of him pre-deceasing me – to read out this, my last will and testament, in the presence of those expressly summoned hereto.

I leave the proceeds of my Prudential Life Insurance Policy to my three daughters: Mrs Jennifer Elliot, Mrs Pauline Thompson and Mrs Julie Anderson. The final amount is to be divided equally by Mr Hertzberg who I have requested to administer this process. The related papers are in his keeping.

To my two Grandsons, Master David Thompson and Master Frank Anderson, who I love dearly, I leave what remains of Mr Gerald Anthony Sumpter's earthly possessions and the sum of £1000 each. Again, this will be administered by Mr Hertzberg who has access to the relevant bank account and records.

To Miss Claire Anderson I leave the sum of £1000 in trust. This will be held in the form of bonds until such time as it is needed or she reaches the age of 18 years old. The office of Mr Hertzberg will administer these bonds until such time and/or representation is made by Miss Claire Anderson's parents.

To Miss Paulette James I leave my gold rose-petal broach and Grandad's Chinese rice bowl. Please cherish it – he wanted you to have it. As you know it was with him when he was a Japanese prisoner of war. I also leave you the sum of £1000. This will be administered by Mr Hertzberg who has access to the relevant bank account.

To Mr Damien Walsh I leave my thanks and appreciation for many years of favours and putting up with a miserable old lady. I also leave the Garage 17f, Rainham Road South RM10 8YP and the contents therein. I hope you enjoy yourself, you deserve it. Thank you a million times for all you have done for me and my family.

To my dear friend Mrs Gertrude Mathews: dry your eyes love, I am in a better place. I leave you my love as always, as well as all the items currently located on my mantelpiece at home, I know you will enjoy them as much as I have. I also leave you my silver ball gown for old times' sake. In addition Mr Hertzberg will consult with you regarding a different matter after today is over.

To Mr Tony Elliot I leave the portrait of my late husband, Mr Gerald Anthony Sumpter. This is located above my mantelpiece at home. Tony, I want you to take a good long look at the picture so you can know what a real man looks like. I regret the day my daughter married you. You have brought her nothing but grief. I hope she finds the nerve to divorce you. To Mr Tony Elliot I have nothing further to say but that the truth will come out. You can't keep your dirty secrets forever.

The remainder of my earthly goods, including my property located at number 22 Warley Avenue, Dagenham RM8 1JU and all remaining sums of monies currently in my bank and building society accounts, I leave to my granddaughter, Miss Janet Sumpter.

Janet, you are to listen to the advice of Mr Hertzberg. He has been a good friend to the family over the years and he helped your Grandad when he needed it. So I trust he will do well by you, (he's got me to answer to if he doesn't). If he's reading this out then you know he got a good nature and he is not as bad as he looks.

You are not to listen to anything your Auntie, Pauline Thompson, has to say on this matter. I know Julie and Jennifer will honour my wishes. It is for the best. I don't wish you to sell the house until you are at least 25 years old. I expect you to go to college and university and make a life for yourself – you deserve it. Damien will help you with anything you need doing and Gertie Mathews can tell you why I am doing this. So be strong girl. What was it they use to tell you at school? *"Every woman has just so much time to live and she can use it or waste it as she wills."*

Pauline, I am sorry to have to say this but you are to leave Janet alone to let her get on with her life as you get on with yours. I hope you can be happy with the money. Jennifer, I only wish I could have been of more help to you love but I know you are strong enough alone. I hope you find peace and contentment. Julie, I know you will be ok whatever you decide to do. I love you all and wish you the best in what you do. God bless and keep you.'

At 18 years old, Janet Sumpter had a very youthful appearance, but was more like a mature woman in a younger body. She had shoulder length brown hair and was about 5ft 9ins with a slight, athletic frame. She gave off a blank expression that many mistook for a serious air, maybe slightly aloof. From a distance she appeared confident. Men took this as a challenge; women she didn't know tended to see her as a threat.

For as long as she could remember, early morning had been Janet's favourite time of day. In Dagenham, when the sun was shining and the air crisp, she would come alive and go for runs on Beacontree Heath. She felt her body warm up and become animated as she stretched and pulled her muscles, her tendons resisting and then finally bending under the pressure of her gentle but firm manipulations. This was a secret pleasure for her. I suppose we always enjoy what we truly control. And for Janet this was 100 per cent her. No-one forced her to run. For that matter no-one encouraged her to run either.

Throughout her school days Janet found Dagenham to be a gloriously down to earth place. She had an epiphany once during a PE lesson. Running was liberating, and even fun. In fact, this liberating experience was the main thing that she enjoyed at school. Her memories of Bob Clack Comprehensive, which she attended until she was 16, were vivid. She had the good times spent with her mates, but more important than anything she had learnt that she enjoyed running. Janet was able to look at life as a race. If she didn't like a particular situation she found herself in, her response was to put as much distance as possible between herself and the problem so that she could get on with what she needed to do.

One spring morning all the girls from form 5GD lined up for the cross-country run during PE. Janet had managed to get out of the three previous figure eights and cross-country runs. It was amazing what you could get away with by saying you had some cramps. That morning she had forgotten all about the cross-country run. She had been having such a great time talking about what was on TV the night before. By the time she twigged that it was cross-country she was already changed into her PE kit. She tried to fake a stomach cramp but Mr Bolton was onto her like a flash. Ninety minutes later she would never be the same person again.

When she got older the more Janet saw of life the more she thought of life in Dagenham as growing up in a different time. Her family didn't have much to speak of. All the families she knew were the same. Back then all of the families down her street were white, British and working class. You see Barking and Dagenham was the former industrial heartland of London. Back then it was a bleak place where East End gangsters lived and relived the glory days of the Krays and the other gangland players. But for Janet, it was the people that made Dagenham worthwhile. For the people that lived there, Dagenham was a village or a small town, not a small part of a great metropolis. The characters that you met on the high street or in the shops made Barking and Dagenham what it was back then and they still make it what it is today. Once you were accepted you felt a part of something tangible and worth preserving.

After Grandma Sumpter died, all the members of the Sumpter clan got a letter from the offices of Jonathan Hertzberg MA LLB NP: Janet's mother Jennifer, her husband Tony and her two sisters Pauline and Julie, Janet's sister Paulette, and her cousins David, Claire and Frank. When they got to the solicitor's office Damien Walsh, a friend of the family, and Mrs Gertie Mathews, Gran's best friend, were also there waiting. Grandma Sumpter had it all worked out. Turns out Mr Hertzberg and Grandma Sumpter went back years. He had been a junior at the law firm when young Mr and Mrs Sumpter bought their house. Back then he was a spotty clerk and Mrs Sumpter was a beautiful young married woman. It turns out there was a lot about Grandma Sumpter that the family didn't know.

Mr Hertzberg cleared his throat once everyone had found a seat. While they were making themselves comfortable he studied the assembled group. He felt he knew each person well, which of course he did thanks to the intimate nature of the conversations he had conducted with Mrs Sumpter over the years. However this was the first time he had met them face to face.

Mr Hertzberg felt very old, especially at times like this. Mrs Sumpter who had died at 84 years of age, was one of the few remaining people who knew him from day one. It amazed him how much Janet Sumpter and Mrs Sumpter were alike, not just in features but in mannerism and posture as well.

Mr Hertzberg wore a classic pinstriped suit, tailored with the kind of detail you would expect from a Saville Row bespoke tailor. It was a very elegant suit that fitted the man well and the room he was in. Mr Hertzberg didn't come across as the handsome type. He didn't have chiselled good looks. His eyes were stern headmaster's eyes that penetrated the subject and looked deep into the person. He had used these tools of the trade to good effect over the years.

After the will reading was over Mr Hertzberg quietly made an appointment with Janet Sumpter. He suggested that she returned in two weeks' time to finalise matters. Afterwards the family headed back to Janet's mother's home. There was silence in all the cars as they headed back. Janet's mum, Jennifer, went to the kitchen and put the kettle on, then thought better of it and took out a half empty bottle a vodka and tray of ice from the freezer. Julie and Tony walked in together. They watched Jennifer drain the contents of the glass in her hand, then they all waited quietly, looking like three rabbits caught in the headlights of an oncoming car. Julie's husband, Peter, was the next to arrive with Janet and the kids. When the front door slammed all hell broke loose. Pauline was on a full rampage; she was f'ing and blinding left right and centre. But Julie and Jennifer stuck to their guns and said they were going to honour their mother's wishes. Janet ended up walking out and staying at a friend's house.

Two weeks later, when Janet went to meet her Grandma's solicitor, Mr Hertzberg outlined the discussions that had taken place between the late Mrs Sumpter and himself. Janet soon realised that her Grandma had trusted Mr Hertzberg a great deal and she decided that she was going to do the same. Mr Hertzberg had a plan of action. As soon as Janet showed willing he set everything in motion.

Janet missed her Grandma dearly. Somehow, speaking with Mr Hertzberg was comforting. Mr Hertzberg suggested that Janet wait until she was 21 before she did anything radical with the house or the money. He then talked her through a full plan of how she could make the most of the opportunity the house presented. Mr Hertzberg said the money that she had was not much of a nest egg but it was a good enough start. Janet agreed to his suggestions.

It wasn't long before Janet was introduced to a man called Mr Singh. Mr Hertzberg had known him for more than 30 years and knew that he was the person that could help Janet with her situation. Mr Maya Singh was the first non-white person Janet had ever had a conversation with. Together with Mr Hertzberg they had viewed three flats in the local area; she now sat with him by her side as she listened attentively to what Mr Maya Singh had to say. By the end of the meeting Janet had signed an agreement to rent out her Gran's house with Mr Singh's letting agency guaranteeing rent for three years. Mr Singh had also helped her complete a mortgage application for the second flat that she had seen that day.

After six weeks she had the keys to her new place and she moved in. There she was, 18 years old, with a house with no mortgage that was rented out. The rent payed the mortgage on the flat she lived in and gave her a monthly income that more than meet her needs.

Mr Hertzberg's next idea was for her to go to university. She didn't see how that was going to work because her grades had been bad. But true to form, she found herself in another meeting discussing her grades with Mr Hertzberg right by her side. He organised for her to redo her Maths and English GCSEs at a private college over the summer. She followed this with a one year Access course for her degree in business and finance. The subject of her degree was Mr Hertzberg's decision. When he had asked her what she wanted to do she had said, 'I don't know' he had looked at her strangely. 'Are you sure you're related to Mary Sumpter?' was his only comment.

The next time Mr Hertzberg asked Janet the same question she had completed her Access course successfully and secured a place at the East London University. Janet spoke with such confidence that it made Mr Hertzberg smile.

'Business, I want to go into business for myself.'

'Ok, what kind of business do you want to get into,' he said.

Without skipping a beat Janet said, 'the property business'.

By the time Janet finished university with a 2.1 in Business and Finance she had nine properties in her portfolio all rented out courtesy of Mr Maya Singh, as well as her flat and her Gran's house. She was only 22. By the time she celebrated her 25th birthday she had a portfolio worth over £3m.

Janet watched Dagenham grow into a truly diverse community. With the regeneration money that was pumped into the borough things just kept improving. Damien Walsh had done some work for her on some of the houses. He kept her in touch with everything that was happening with her family.

She met her mum for the first time after four years at the funeral of Mrs Gertrude Mathews. They sat down in a cafe after the service. Jennifer was full of questions. 'So, how have things been with you Janet. I've missed you. Why haven't you been in touch with me all this time?

'Mum, you know how Auntie Pauline was,' said Janet. 'It was never-ending. Her only agenda was to get the house from me. I just couldn't take it any more so I just decided that I needed to get on with my life, which is what Gran wanted.'

'I see. But do you know that your sister had a baby and me and Tony got divorced,' said Jennifer.

'I heard about the baby but not about your divorce. I heard Tony walked out, but no, not about the divorce. What did Paulette have, a boy or girl?'

'She had a boy. Don't you care about the fact that I had a divorce?'

'I reckon that it was about time. Gran said you should have divorced him in her will. I don't know why you stayed married to him for so long,' Janet retorted.

'You could show some sympathy.'

'Not when it involves Tony.'

'Damien tells me that you are doing alright for yourself.'

'What's that supposed to mean?'

'Don't you know the state the family is in?' Jennifer asked. 'Don't you know what happened to Auntie Pauline last year and Auntie Julie and the kids? Have you not heard about their situation?'

'No, I don't know what happened to anybody. I've just been getting on with my life. No-one has been in touch with me to let me know anything that is going on,' said Janet. 'Listen Mum, I never asked Gran to leave me the house. We never ever had any conversations about it. All the stuff that Auntie Pauline is saying, that I convinced Gran to leave me the house before she died is nonsense. You do believe me don't you?'

'Of course I know it's nonsense. She was my mum you know. Me and Julie know that what Pauline is saying doesn't hold water. You shouldn't worry about things. That's just Pauline trying to get her own way. She's always been a spoilt brat.'

'Do you want to know why I think Gran left me the house?'

'Of course.'

'Me and Gran had an understanding. We never talked about things openly. But she always knew what was happening. She had a way of guessing things and letting me know that she knew. You know how she was.'

'Yes, go on, what did she find out?'

At this point, tears welled up in Janet's eyes as she looked into her mum's face for any clues about what she knew. But Jennifer only stared blankly at her daughter waiting in anticipation for what Janet had to say.

'Well it going to sound weird but it's Gertie who filled in the blanks for me. I went to see her a few times after Gran's will reading. You know that Gran had organised for her and Mr Mathews to go on a cruise as well as to have the stuff on her mantelpiece? Well, the first time I saw her, she was all excited. Turns out they had been saving for a cruise for 10 years but had to use the money a few times. Mr Mathews had to wait for the OK from the doctor's, due to his heart condition. The day I went around to see her. The doctor had called in the morning giving the OK. They had called and told Mr Hertzberg. Which, apparently was the arrangement they had. When I got there Gertie was on the phone to him – he had called to tell them that their passage was booked on the cruise leaving in a week's time. Well I didn't get much sense out of her then but she made me promise to come and see her when she and Mr Mathews got back.'

'Go on what happened, what did she say?'

'Well,' Janet continued. 'Three months later I was meeting Damien Walsh round by Grandad's garage, when I got a call from Gertie on my mobile. Gertie was asking if I could come to see her that day. Damien gave me a lift in Grandad's car that was in the garage that Gran had left him in the will. He had spruced it up and was showing it off – Gertie said it looked better than new. Anyway Gertie said that Gran had the idea for the will, including what she wanted me to do with my life. because of that film that I used to watch all the time. You remember the one mum, *Sliding Doors*. Gertie said that Gran wanted me to have the chance at life that she never had. The chance that she couldn't provide for her daughters due to times being so hard when she and Grandad was raising them. Turns out Gran was quite bright in her day was offered a place at university but never went due to her getting pregnant with Auntie Pauline. I never knew about that until Gertie told me, but Gran and Grandad got married after they found out.'

'Well I never heard that one before. Mum never mentioned anything like that. Are you sure Gertie knew what she was talking about?'

'Mr Mathews was Grandad's best man and Gertie was Gran's bridesmaid, so Gran tell Gertie that if she goes first she is to tell me everything and help me move on with my life. Listen mum, Mr Hertzberg, Gran's solicitor, he's a diamond. He's helped me a lot over the past few years and now with Gertie gone it made me think about our family. I need your help mum. Gran had a plan. There is a lot to tell you about. Damien was right, I am doing alright and it's about time I fulfilled my promise to Gran.'

Both women knew that they needed to be in a space where they could continue what had just taken place. So together they left the cafe and made their way back home to Jennifer's house.

Paulette and Janet had a tearful reunion and the three women talked through the night. Paulette talked about how tough things had been over the past few years due to her husband gambling away all their money. Tony had cleaned out mum's bank account before he disappeared. Auntie Julie had put Frank and Claire into a private school and had now run out of money as well. Early the next day, Janet borrowed some of Paulette's clothes and went for a run.

As she ran through Beacontree Heath she marvelled at how much Dagenham had changed in the time she had been away. She noticed the Asian and black families doing the school run. The sunlight was dancing across the rooftops and the trees. As she looked down towards the town centre she noticed the new buildings. As she ran she felt the embrace of the community calling her home. She realised that she didn't need to run away from anything anymore. She remembered why Dagenham was such a great place to live.

By the time she got back to her mum's she had decided what she was going to do for her family. Her dear Grandma had given her an opportunity in life, now it was time for her to help her family and fulfil the promise she had made to her Gran. Something Bob Clack used to say rang in her ears, *'Every woman has just so much time to live and she can use it or waste it as she wills.'*

REDBRIDGE

The Homecoming

The Homecoming

Deborah O'Connor

My thirteen year old sister was pregnant and it was all my fault. That's what I expected mum to say anyway.

I wasn't sure if the tongue-lashing would begin as soon as I opened the front door or if she would let me unpack my things first. Either way, I knew that when her anger did come, it would be thick, fast and probably leave a mark.

Whatever. Under my breath, I began rehearsing the accent and turns of phrase she would be expecting of me, tongue-lashing or not. But the Essex twang was harder than I remembered and I kept stumbling over the vowels and dropped consonants that would blend me back in.

The taxi came to a stop at some traffic lights and I found myself sitting parallel to the queue for the town's biggest club, Funkymojoes. At Heathrow the sky had been full of drizzle but, as we had travelled from west to east, the rain had turned to snow. Here, in South Woodford, I saw that a thick layer of white had crusted itself onto the pavements and that the Friday night contingent had been undeterred by the new and forbidding clime. With a pride I didn't understand, I smiled at the skilled way their polished black loafers and spiky heels navigated the icy walkways, and the way the girls braved the arctic terrain with only their sun-bed tans and polyester mini dresses for warmth.

I stared at them, trying to remember, trying to will myself back to something, a feeling I couldn't quite place. I looked up to the criss-crossed Christmas light strings decorating the air; a cat's cradle of wire and bulb stars, snowmen and angels that seemed to be all that was stopping the High Road from collapsing in on itself. But it was no good. No matter how hard I concentrated on the queue and the lights, that feeling, I couldn't quite reach it.

My last phone conversation with mum had been a few nights ago. I'd had her on speaker so that I could talk and listen at the same time as I tried to cram all the Christmas presents I'd bought (and a few of my clothes) into one suitcase. She'd been warbling on about nothing much – the X-Factor finals, her freezer going on the blink, the dog's favourite new chew-toy – when something she said had snagged on my ear like a nail on a new pair of tights. I put down the Empire State snow-globes I was trying to wedge in amongst my cashmere jumpers and picked up the phone.

As she'd gone on to feel her way around words like *new addition* and *little acciden*t, and bumbled into allusions about *finding out too late,* I'd began to understand what she was trying to tell me. To be honest, I wasn't that surprised. I knew that in the last year lots of girls in Leanne's school had fallen pregnant and that some had kept the babies and some hadn't. No, what had made me bristle was the way that mum had qualified everything she said with lines that were full of blame, lines like *you haven't been here have you love?...with your family where you belong... we've missed you... you're Leanne's big sister... my firstborn.* That and the way she kept harping on about how wonderful Vince had been through the whole ordeal, *I can always rely on Vince* (Vince was the landlord of the local pub and a family friend).

Leanne getting pregnant. It felt inevitable somehow. I knew that if I hadn't got out when I did, it could have been me staring one of those blue pee stick lines in the face. But luck or fate or chance or whatever you want to call it had intervened. One minute I was wandering around Topshop in my lunch hour, the next I was being scouted for a modelling job. I knew that and I was thankful for it. I comforted myself with the fact that mum was still young – barely forty – and so would be able to help Leanne with the baby so that she could at least finish school.

The taxi was out of the town centre and nearly there. The driver turned left at the bruised and battered remains of the old BT telephone exchange that marked the start of mum's estate, my old estate (when had I started thinking of it as belonging to mum?) and I saw how its smashed windows had finally been boarded over. Each square of the cheap hamburger wood was swollen with old rain. Despite the weather and the darkness, lads in silky blue tracksuit bottoms were playing football in the exchange's locked car park, none of them yet old enough to while away their benefit in the pub over the road.

The taxi turned right at the clumpy pebble-dash bungalow that marked the avenue and I saw how some of the houses wore snug metal grilles on their windows. Mum had spent another one of her (very expensive) long distance phone calls telling me in great detail about how the men from the council had come to fix them up all on the same day. These were the houses nobody lived in any more. As we cruised down the road, me directing the driver to the right door number, the houses got better. These had their Christmas trees up and their curtains kept open so that the fairy lights and red and gold tinsel sellotaped to picture frames and fireplaces, could be admired from the street.

I paid the driver and was lugging my suitcase out of the boot when Leanne's face appeared in the thin gap allowed by the door while the chain was still in the bolt. She gave me a smile before shutting the door again to free it, and then tip-toed barefoot onto the concrete step to give me a hug. I tried to feel for the beginnings of a baby bump but she had her fleecy trackies on and so I couldn't really tell. Maybe she was only a few months gone.

I went inside and into the small pocket of heat that was the front room. The gas fire was on full and next to it, in her favourite armchair, was mum, doing her lipsticks. Instinctively, I looked for that other familiar shape, a tiny figure tucked into the corner of the sofa. And there she was, Nanna Black, her hands folded blankly on her knees.

As Leanne shut the door and rearranged the sausage-dog draft excluder, I went over to give mum a kiss hello, but she didn't get up; wouldn't meet my eyes even. This was going to be worse than I thought.

I made a token lean in towards Nanna, not wanting to frighten her and certainly not expecting my greeting to be reciprocated. But, to my surprise, she smiled as though she recognised me and reached up to hold my face like I was a lover, her smooth hands veiny and dry. With shaky lips she said my name, 'Julie,' and I stood back in shock.

'She's having a good day today,' explained mum without looking up from her lipsticks. 'Must be in honour of your coming all this way home. Enjoy it while it lasts. Normally she thinks I'm some stranger come to rape and burgle her. All at the same time. Don't you mum?'

Nanna Black patted the space next to her on the sofa.

'Home is where the heart is,' she said looking me right in the eye, as though it was the most revelatory, most new, most important message in the world. I sagged. This, among other things was something I knew that Nanna said over and over, at random and meaningless points, and her saying it meant that the lucidity I'd just witnessed (or thought I'd witnessed) was gone.

I sat down next to Nanna and braced myself for mum to start ranting. I guessed it would go something along the lines of, *This would never have happened if you hadn't gone away* and would be followed by something about how her precious Leanne had rebelled *because you weren't there when she needed you.* And indeed, how I might as well have been the one that led her up the stairs at a dodgy party, got her to lay on a bed and invited the first acne-ridden moron I could find to do the down and dirty with her.

But, contrary to my predictions, mum was mute and so I turned my attentions to Nanna who (excited at having company) was motioning for me to pass her the enormous photograph album that rested at her feet. The album contained all the pictures of our cousin Nicola's wedding. I knew from mum that the album had been Nan's new favourite thing for a good few months, even though Nicola had been married almost ten years. It was enormous. Covered in red stitched leather, it came in a specially designed briefcase that took such an effort to heave down from the cabinet that mum had taken to leaving it lying around permanently in what was her otherwise immaculate house.

Tapping me on the arm to get my attention, Nan opened the album with a happy sigh. It was full of all the usual wedding shots: the bride (Nicola) with her dimpled upper arms and tonged curls of hair in poses on a bench, kissing her groom, turning around coyly in a picture designed to show off her excessive ivory train. It was all pretty standard stuff, but somehow, no matter how many times I saw it, I always got fixated on the fact that, in some of the important set piece shots, cousin Nicola had her eyes closed. But as Mum said, they'd agreed a price that allowed them only a limited amount of frames and they couldn't afford to pay for any more, so 'Even if the snaps weren't as perfect as perfect can be,' they'd gone ahead and put them in the album anyway, 'Otherwise we'd have been left without a full set, wouldn't we now?'

I thought of the set of photos I now had. All perfectly lit, some had me sporting a washed-out, meow-meow chic look, while others had me as an all-American girl, smiling whitely in Ralph Lauren linens. A couple of them had me as a Helmut Newton-esque nude (all glamazonian legs, oiled up skin and super contrasting blacks and whites). I had, of course, made sure not to tell mum about these. To think of her ever seeing me like that. My legs apart. Defiant in high heels. The expression on my face. What was it my friends always said? 'As far as your parents are concerned, neither you nor they have ever, ever had sex'. They would concede the obvious reproductive flaw in their delusion and then shudder over-dramatically and say, 'Because what's the alternative?'

Back in New York, I would carry this set of photos around with me all day on the subway. Contained in my book (a big black plastic folder with the agency's name on the side) the pictures charted the staging posts of my new life in perfect matte detail. Starting with my first, ultra-gauche wedding dress shots (all new models were sent to Japan to do the obligatory bridal work), flick forward a few pages and you were into the slightly sassier stuff, a campaign I'd done for H&M (a campaign I'd won after cutting and bleaching my long brown hair short), a D-Squared jeans advert. Towards the end of the book, before the blank cellophane pockets waiting to be filled, was my more recent, high-end glossy work. In these photos my beauty had been routinely bludgeoned by bizarre hairstyles, over-size eyebrows and eccentric make-up. Bludgeonings that would make Leanne declare (when she eventually saw the pics in magazines) that I looked 'totally minging'.

Nan had had enough of Nicola's wedding album and so I put it back by her feet. It was about the same weight as my book. Fresh off the plane as I was, the thought of going back to it and the endless go-sees that now made up my day made me feel tired. But I also knew that, given a few days here, the thought of my tiny studio apartment, the hub and bub that was the catwalk and the sight of models backstage, lifting up their faces to the make-up artists like babies wanting to be fed, would make me regret agreeing to mum's demand that I stay for the entire Christmas holidays.

I relaxed into the cushions and began acquainting myself with mum's latest colour scheme. Fiercely proud of her front room, she considered it the show-piece of the house and redecorated it every year. This year I knew she'd saved hard for some wallpaper from Next and that Vince had helped her to put it up ('There's no way you'd ever get me up those stepladders. Oh no'). On the bottom half of the wall was the first kind of paper, embossed pink and cream stripes edged with gold, interrupted halfway up by a fat border of vertical paper that acted as a kind of two-dimensional dado rail. Then, on the top half of the wall (in the same colour scheme) was the second kind of paper, a simple diamond design. Even though I knew my new meatpacking district sensibility should mean that it made me cringe, in reality, being back here, with the garish décor, tiny warm spaces and old school photos on the mantelpiece, I felt safe. I knew I would sleep well tonight. If I wanted to, I thought, I could come back to all of this. I imagined what it would feel like, to stop fighting it and just give in. Would it be like shutting your eyes and letting go?

'How was your flight? Do you fancy a sandwich? I've got some of that nice Tesco's Finest loaf' asked Mum, fishing another fistful of lipsticks out of the bag and onto her lap.

So this was how it was going to be. Maybe she had decided to play nice until Nanna went to bed and then she would start the flogging.

'No thanks. I'm alright, I had something on the plane,' I lied, taking off my heels. Even though she'd offered, I knew the tell-tale signs of her being behind on a big order when I saw them (Leanne sat helping her, the TV turned up loud to cover the sound of the clicking) and so I didn't want to distract her from the job in hand.

Mum had started doing the lipsticks when Leanne and I were little. It didn't pay as well as working at a check-out or something like that, but it did mean that she could be home when we got in from school and could look after us if we were ever poorly. Each Monday, a man in a van would drop off ten huge clear bags full of unmade plastic pieces and she would hoist them all into the back kitchen; the noise of the plastic shifting around like the clackiest of hail-stone storms. Her job was to put each piece into its final designated shape: a tube mechanism that operated lipsticks up and down from inside. She'd organised her mini-production line in the same way for years: keeping the fresh bag to the left of her arm-chair – with its hundreds upon hundreds of tubes with their thin slits down the middle – and the bag full of finished products on the other side, ready for Cherry Sunset or Magenta Dawn to be poured into them at the factory at the end of the week.

They looked like those over-complicated toys you sometimes find inside Kinder eggs, the kind you break within seconds, but Mum had been doing them for so long that she didn't even need to look down when she worked; her hands expertly popping and clicking each bit of plastic together while she watched *Emmerdale* or *Eastenders*.

'Them kids have been at it again,' she said launching into the kind of conversation that presumed I was around all the time and so would know what she was talking about. 'They've only been piddling through people's letter-boxes. On a morning as well, when there's a pile of post sat right there.' Nanna Black nodded enthusiastically as though she knew all about it and said, 'There's no place like home.'

Mum stopped and looked at her open-mouthed, but then her patience, fine-tuned from years of having to deal with random interjections like this, kicked in and she carried on. 'Then the other day they only went and set fire to Rita next door's shopping bags while she was waiting for the bus in town.'

When mum wasn't looking, Leanne gestured with her eyes toward the bedroom upstairs, her bare feet grinding into the thick carpet and disturbing the perfect, lawn-like lines that Mum created daily by pushing the vacuum cleaner from one side of the room to the other. It seemed she wanted to tell me her side of the story before mum could poison me with her version of events.

'Julie!' mum said, trying to draw my attention back to her. ' Julie Black, I'm talking to you. I know we might not be as interesting as all your fancy new New York friends but I, your mother, was speaking to you,' she scolded.

'Sorry mum, I was...'

'And when your mother is speaking to you, you listen!' she declared. I tried not to scream.

'Oh don't look at me with those big doe-eyes. You're just like your dad you are,' she said, closing in on herself the way she did whenever she felt she'd been snubbed, 'constantly looking over someone's shoulder for the next best thing.'

Dad. He used to drive the lorries. Long-haul. Mum said that it was good money but bad for his back. I didn't remember that much about him except for the little things. Things like how he used to come home from the pub, the outsides of his leather jacket deliciously cold on my cheek when I hugged him, the inside pockets lined with bags of crisps for me and Leanne; his voice thick with drink and love. Or how, on New Year's Eve, he would lift me onto his shoulders so that we could go up and down the street letting the New Year in.

'Leanne, did you tell your sister about Auntie Sue?' Mum asked, her fingers working extra fast. My previous transgression was apparently forgiven. I watched as she felt intuitively for the right places to bend and slot and fix, and (where necessary) use brute force to achieve the required shape.

When Leanne didn't respond to her prompt she kept going.

'She's got a new caravan. You wanna see it Julie. Massive it is,' she enthused. 'Had it specially built she did. It was so massive they had to transport it down the motorway to Southend in the middle of the night. They had to have two police escorts. Two.' She laughed to herself. 'Oh it's beautiful inside, isn't it our Leanne? Bee-you-ti-ful' she said, relishing each syllable. 'The bathroom. It's got a sink, it's got a toilet, it's got a shower.' She went to go on with her list but then interrupted herself. 'Not one of those showers in the bath mind you, like we have. A separate one. And they've got one of those round baths with the bubbles in it. A... a...?'

'A jacuzzi' said Leanne, her quick jump-in revealing that she'd answered this question before.

'Yeah, a jacuzzi,' she said, taking a gulp of her tea, her eyes lost in thought at the thing, readying herself for the task of describing each and every room of the caravan in turn. The finished pile of lipsticks on her right was almost up to her elbows, the other side nearly finished. Refreshed, she carried on.

'It's got two massive settees and a wide-screen telly in the front room and a lovely gas oven in the kitchen. And in the bedroom, loads of wardrobes, loads of storage. All fitted mind you.'

Leanne gave me another look and this time I decided to meet her gaze, my sign that I was now ready to give in and let her spill the beans. Leanne leapt up in excitement, and then, remembering herself, feigned a yawn.

'God I'm wrecked. Do you mind if I leave the rest of the lipsticks for you Mum? I'm ready to drop.' She went over and kissed the top of her head. I followed suit.

'Me too. It's been a long day. Jet-lag and all that.'

I was almost at the top of the stairs when Mum shouted me back.

'Julie love, can you come back in here a tick?'

From where she stood on the landing Leanne shook her head and mouthed a 'No' at me. I knew she would huff and puff if I didn't follow her into the bedroom but what was I supposed to do? I hadn't seen mum since the summer and besides, I figured, it was better to get my bollocking out of the way. Then at least we could start tomorrow afresh.

'I'm sorry Lee, I'll be up in a minute, I promise,' I said, reaching over to ruffle her blonde crop before going back down the stairs two at a time. I hovered at the doorway but Mum motioned for me to come in.

'Shut the door love.'

On the sofa, I saw that Nanna Black was asleep. Laid on her side, she was snuffling quietly into the cushions. I sat down and began stroking her baby chick-like silver hair. I decided to beat Mum to the punch. I was tired and I'd decided that I was sick of her finding a way to blame me for things that weren't my fault.

'Look, I know what you're going to say and it's not fair mum, really it isn't. I know I went away, far away, but it was too good an opportunity to miss. You know that, you even said it yourself. I'm sorry it's been hard for you, hard for Leanne, really, I am. But if you're going to start saying that what's happened to her is my fault, that her getting knocked up is something to do with me, well that's just not right...' I was still speaking when mum stood up from her armchair. The mound of lipsticks that had been obscuring her lap clattered to the floor.

'Julie,' she said, her voice all hard and quiet. 'Me and Vince, well, we thought I was too old you see, but then...'

'Mum?'

And then she turned so that she was facing me side-on and lifted her jumper. The skin across her rounded belly was already so taut that, in places it was almost translucent.

'Julie, please don't be mad.'

NEWHAM

A Village by Any Other Name

A Village by Any Other Name

Kadija Sesay

A limousine was trying to gain access to Memorial Avenue. It stretched across the mini-roundabout blocking the pathway of all three exits. People exiting the underground station looked on and stared, bewildered. Those leaning against the back of the street benches, hands in pockets, turned and stared intently, something to take up their interest through the boredom of waiting for their ride. Some of them huffed:

''e's 'avin' a larf!'

The assumption was it was either a lost driver or an important 'somebody' come to 'pop in' to the new sports centre at the end of the road. People moving in and out of the underground just shook their heads; people who hung around pointed and jeered with some choice words in different dialects and languages:

'What a nonce – eh!'

'Look pan de fool.'

'Oh my days!'

The chaos that the long vehicle created even brought out halal chippie from behind his grill during a busy lunch hour to light a ciggy and have a nose.

'Wha's going on?' he said in Cockney Arabic dialect as he lit up.

'Must be opening the new sport centre – no one else would be so daft as to bring a car like that 'ere.'

'Whose openin' it then? Don' remember seeing anythin' abou-it, like.'

'Mayor,' two people said in unison.

'What, Boris? Nah, he'd be on his bike!'

Everyone in earshot on the pavement laughed loudly and falsely.

'Nah! 'E'd be scared someone would nick it dan-ere, but you can't see inside, can ya?'

'Must be red as a beetroot or wearin' a red nose with all this malarkey he's creating. Whaddya reckon?'

'I reckon it's a waste of bloody time an' money meself – not like it's for the Olympics is it?'

They looked at each other again, this time not laughing but questioning.

'Didn't think about that! Maybe it is an' we just haven't been told.'

Halal chippie went back in and the others moved on, as the limo finally began to manoeuvre into the tight space and pulled to the side to let an oncoming yellow smart car pass.

'Now, that's what he should be coming down 'ere in – the only thing that can move around 'ere!'

The limousine moved up – eyes followed slowly. Gone were the days when kids would chase the limousine, with sticks for legs and in their hands, as these days they were chided if they played in the streets, so the plush black vehicle moved on unhindered.

But Mark, the café owner, kept that thought in his mind – something about the Olympics? Who was opening the new sports centre? Hadn't it already been opened? What was going on there? Did they need catering – they should be using someone local like me!

It was tough having a café in weepy West Ham. He had thought that with the new Transport for London development, people would at least come in and sit down and have a cuppa while waiting, but it didn't happen that much. He also wanted to be well-placed for the Olympic rush.

It was only a small arcade of shops – a bit busier now that the underground had expanded sufficiently so that it mattered; he remembered as a teenager signing the campaign to keep the Post Office open. They failed. Now the nearest one was a bus or train ride in either direction to Stratford or Canning Town. For a small late-night business like his, this was not comfortable. It meant that he either had to leave his takings on the premises overnight or take them with him as there were no banks nearby either. Didn't think of that, did they – idiots – helping small businesses? Yeah, right! How was the area supposed to develop with no business facilities?

He had often thought of giving up the café on that little strip. It was frequented only by locals, who in the main didn't work, although sometimes people popped in if they were waiting for someone to pick them up. It was frustrating, but hopefully waiting for local Olympic traffic would encourage them to stay on. They were promised all sorts of things and how it was going to be good for the area – good for them – they could only benefit come 2012. He would have people queuing outside, the local Olympic Committee spokesperson said, West Ham station will be one of the three 'gateway' stations to the Olympic Park – and yeah – till then? What incentives were they offering till then? How would they survive until then?

He had opened another café, hoping that the one in East Ham, much busier, would support the income of the Rial Lifestyle Café in West Ham till that time, but it was tight, touch and go, as even though there was more people traffic, there was also more competition, and his slim build was less due to his Filipino background, than for the fact that he was run off his feet working 25/8! But he was still young and he hoped that he had the energy for the next few years to see that it would all be worthwhile and turn him, not into a millionaire but at least make him financially comfortable and maybe, before he was 32, he would be able to buy his own home… that was his dream.

These were his thoughts as the 'swoosh' of the black limo streamed back past again. That was quick! Snip the ribbon, break the champers and gone! He still couldn't believe that someone had come down to 'open' it – he would check it out later, after closing.

He walked past the Memorial Avenue Sports centre on his way home. No sign that any major activity had taken place. He asked his parents but they didn't seem to know anything, and neither did the other shop owners when he asked them the next day. They shook their heads, no-one seemed to remember or care that much.

The strip of shops on the avenue was a mix of the old, the new (the site of the alienated mini-mart opposite the other shops, into which blasted the tanoid on the underground was owned by TfL), so not all of the business owners had the same emotional investment as he and Errol.

So what had the limo been doing there yesterday? Maybe everyone was right and the driver was just lost. But two weeks later, a hand-dropped letter through the door explained the mysterious visit.

Dear Resident,

Congratulations! As a resident of Newham, the Olympic borough, this is an exciting time for you. The area, like your sister borough, Hackney, is being regenerated and you will receive the massive benefits that always comes to Olympic towns.

Yet, our concern is that with the hundreds of thousands of visitors headed your way as the Olympics draws near, that they will become confused that the football club is not at the underground station with the same name. West Ham United Football Club has been in existence, as you know, since 1895 and is part of the pride of Newham, so we are suggesting that West Ham tube station changes its name to one of the names below:

Stratford West
Plaistow East
Canning North
Or you can suggest an alternative here:

Everyone who responds with a suggestion will enter a prize draw. The winner and his/her family will receive one month's free travel throughout the TfL network.

Yours sincerely,

The Mayor of London's Office

P. S. If a clear winning name is not found, then one will be selected by a Mayor of London committee.

They're 'avin a larf!

Are they?

All of a sudden, this didn't sound so funny. They had been given 10 weeks to select a name – or what?

One will be selected.

The next day, Mark went first into Errol's off licence/newsagents even before opening his café.

'Mate, you seen this letter – have you seen it!'

'I'm reading it now… what's it to you …' Errol, the man with the all-day smile, was not smiling.

'I live round here – like you – I was born here – in West Ham! We'll have to change everything!'

'I know. This is ridiculous.'

'So, what do we do?'

'Let's start a campaign.'

Mark smirked, 'Yeah, right.'

Errol looked up, 'What's wrong with a campaign?'

'Remember the Post Office campaign? Where did that get us – eh? And this is something much bigger – has to go much further – do you think they are going to look at our petition?'

'We can try – lets make a start – I'm sure there are loads of people in the area who feel the same as us. All of us who live here, have homes and businesses here, like you and me, we all feel the same.'

'Get the housing on to it as well – its gonna cost them too – and the council.'

'You're right. Changing the name of a town ain't no cheap thing.'

'A town?'

'Yeah, town.'

'West Ham isn't a town.'

'What is it then?'

Mark was honestly lost for words.

'Do you have villages in a borough?'

'You've hit it on the head Mark,' Errol shrugged – what are we?'

'The "forgotten zone".'

'So, is that a reason to give in to what they want?'

'Do they think people round here don't matter, or what?'

'It's our home. Let's start with the petition, anyway man, it's a start.'

'Yeah,' said Mark. 'It's a start.' And a finish, he said silently in his head.

Nothing will really happen with this. There had to be something else. There had to be another way.

Mark and Errol drew up the petition and put it in their shops. They got halal chippie to put it in his and the small grocery store next to it. They wanted to put it in the obvious place, the underground station, but as much as the staff sympathised, they were paid by 'the Man' who wanted to make the change and they shook their heads.

'Volunteers – get volunteers to stand outside the station every morning and every evening, get them to sign this.'

'Who's got mates who work at the council?'

'I do.'

'Get 'em to sign this, will ya?'

'Course.'

Errol was out there with his charming, Jamaican self, upbeat, talking everyone into fighting the name change. Marcia, his wife, smoothly stepped behind the counter, each time he ran out to get another signature. They fitted together like a glove, even looked like each other – one of those 'forever' couples.

They set up a Facebook page – SaveWestHam.

What we need to do, Mark thought, is to get people to recognise West Ham for something famous – not just the stop on the underground – which didn't benefit from being in Zone 3 – and find a way to divert the focus from the 'long illustrious history of the football club'. They couldn't even ask the football club to help their campaign, since in essence they were fighting against it. How do you fight against the local, the national and the international presence of a world-wide name, eh?

And hadn't the powers that be, been clever? The sports facility that housed two football pitches and a rugby pitch, and a soon to be amphitheatre was named after the Road, 'Memorial Avenue', not the area. So, what was West Ham famous for? Apart from the Premier League team that was in Upton Park?

We need something big and newsworthy and whatever it was, something, permanent. He hadn't broached this suggestion to Errol yet; the past experience of their relationship told him that he would just laugh.

He was much younger than Errol and he felt that he really didn't take him seriously as a business person, but if he came up with something that would work ...

They were down to eight weeks before the deadline, which meant seven weeks max. to make something happen.

'Well, the numbers are piling,' Errol said proudly, 'we have 1600 names – that's like nearly half of the households in West Ham. Ain't bad. Whaddya think? People on Springfield Road have signed, Memorial Avenue, Holland Road, Valerian Way, Hamilton Road, Teasel Way, Godbold Road ... everyone on the stretch between here and Canning Town and the flats up the other way toward Stratford. It's great. Yeah, the response has been great!'

'Yeah,' Mark agreed, but it was not enough.

'It's not enough,' the words slipped out.

'You what? Well, what have you done, eh? You were never really in on this from the beginning, were you Mark? You don't really give a shit. All the hard work I've put into this!'

'I just think that we need to do something more ...'

'Like what? Well you come up with something, then!'

'You're right. Give me a week – I'll come up with something in a week but it might help if we can fight this together ...'

'Naa, I'm not 'fighting' with you ... there's no fight in you ...'

The sports link that Mark had originally thought of, trying to get a local athlete into the Olympics was just not going to work. No athletic talent seemed to be forthcoming and 'Rugby Sevens' that the sports centre was also used for, wasn't recognised as an Olympic Sport until the 2016 Summer Olympics in Rio de Janeiro. Mark was getting desperate for ideas. How else could they get on the map?

It was a typical British day that saved them – a rainy, Sunday, summer afternoon – when in a heightened spirit of camaraderie that the issue of the name change had brought to their streets, some West Ham residents decided to hold a yard sale at the Grassroots Community Resource Centre. All the stallholders were ready with plastic sheets to cover their goods, no matter how cheap and seemingly worthless they seemed – someone would buy them.

They decided to hold a 'Save West Ham' meeting, just before the yard sale since so many members of the community would be there. At first, as the meeting was Mark's idea, he wanted to have it at his café, but although it was a comfortable, laid back space, it was far too small for the numbers they hoped and expected would attend. One side of Rial's walls was a montage of polaroids of the Rial's regulars and favourites, with a small collection of Polaroid cameras in their own glass case. There were bookshelves filled with art and design books, from a backlist of *Wallpaper,* Taschen books on interior design in different countries, and a full rare collection of the distinctive black and white SABLE Literary Magazine. People could sit all day inside Rial with a cup of tea, or outside, smoking. But not for the meeting. It was many of those regulars displayed on his walls who had been his ardent supporters in dreaming up a new and wild idea to get West Ham recognised, so it was decided to rendezvous at the café and walk together to the community centre.

Mark hadn't been there before and he had to admit, one of the reasons that he didn't want to hold the meeting at Grassroots was because they had their own café, so he was a bit miffed. But once he saw the community centre, he could see why people raved about it. It was a pretty amazing building, built 'into' the park, with a grass topped roof that turned his face into a picture of admiration. Somebody had told him that it had won a Green Flag Award for its energy saving features and another award for its innovative design and construction. How could anyone believe that West Ham wasn't on the map with a building like this!

It was Errol's charismatic voice that called the meeting to attention.

'Hey people, listen up! Thank you all for signing the petition. And in case you haven't, step over here, its not too late! Guess what? We are gonna add more pizzazz and excitement. To get West Ham on the map, we are going to ask everyone to join us outside City Hall when we present the petition so if you've got any ideas to make this a day to remember, come over and let us know.'

There were mixed murmurs. Most people seemed to be bemused, but a few local residents did come over to listen to what was going on, and a couple more came with whacky suggestions.

Errol turned and nodded at Mark.

'Good thinking, this. Simple, but the meeting today was a good idea.'

One of Mark's regulars turned out to be a volunteer at the Newham Bookshop on Barking Road which had been a landmark in the area for 30 years. The famous 'dread' poet, nicknamed 'The Bard of Newham' lived in the area and was a big supporter of the bookstore. She offered to find out if he wouldn't mind supporting them – they could only try…

She had a PO Box address to contact him that she suspected was more like a Doctor Who thing – that it went into the stratosphere – but what did they have to lose? They had four weeks to go.

Errol followed up on the role he did best – promoting and campaigning – well, Marcia did the work of the promoting and he did the schmoozing of the campaigning. As soon as he and Mark had confirmed date and place, they would let West Ham-onians know.

The success of the campaign with signed names and the possibility of celebrity support made an impressive PR presentation pack for the Mayor's office. Their campaigning Facebook page quadrupled its sign ups within days after the meeting at Grassroots – the momentum was building.

Mark and Errol wanted to make the presentation to the Mayor of London personally – not to a 'representative' or his right hand man; it was important to them and West Ham residents to have media attention.

It needed the Mayor, and a celebrity. Errol's wife, Marcia, had organised the publicity, coordinated the presentation and the day down to a 'T' and made everything click like digital. She had contacted the press, learned how to write an effective press release, with the help of staff at Grassroots, arranged for Newham's local press photographer to be there, found out the rules and legalities for gatherings of mass numbers and checked which days the Mayor would be in. They needed the cameras to be on them, at City Hall not on the Mayor in another part of town or with a visiting dignitary.

Over 200 people arrived at City Hall on the designated day and time, witnessed by the ecstatic whoops, back slapping and arm clutching of Mark and Errol. If this didn't get them press coverage, nothing would. It seemed as though Mark's regular customer had really done her bit and they felt that press coverage was guaranteed when the loping, wide stepping, locks flaying from the 'Bard of Newham', appeared. Their whoops got louder! All cameras turned on him, but no-one cared – he was a faithful community activist who could get them in the papers and hopefully radio and TV, too. 'My poem for West Ham' he stated simply and loudly. And true to his word, he span off a rhyme, to support the cause and to big up Newham.

So, the petition is in, to save the name of the sleepy village/town of West Ham in Zone 3. But they haven't let it rest there ... why should they... no way... this campaign had really stoked their enthusiasm and commitment. Mark and Errol were on a roll ... and the continual push was, what would see West Ham, Zone 3, be on the top line – or at least the first page on Google. They had raised money from the yard sale, so they could possibly pay for that position, but what else?

A West Ham – The Cocktail (Errol's idea).

The West Ham Wrap (Mark's favourite idea)

West Ham residents break a *Guinness Book of Records* world record (which one?)

Walking Drawings, West Ham? The latest community pitch seemed to be The Big Art or The Big Draw and one resident came up with an idea that she'd seen on the telly, to have a 'Walking Drawing' in Memorial Park, which all the residents could participate in. Now that would attract media attention, she said proudly.

The suggestions became larger, more ambitious and more outrageous. The ideas were put together to create a new photographic artpiece that Rial Café put up on its wall.

The latest idea on the list so far, on the community board outside Rial Café was to bring West Ham United Football Ground back home to West Ham – to Memorial Park, the first and true home of the football club. Although someone had scribbled over it – 'Forget the Club, just give us a Post Office!'

The deadline to hear about the outcome of the name change came and went… in the meantime, at the rear of Errol's off-licence, West Ham got its Post Office. That in itself will guarantee that West Ham, stays as West Ham.

WALTHAM FOREST
North by North East

North by North East

Ashleigh Lezard

Two Days Earlier

The hangover felt like a drill was screwing into his brain. He blinked as his eyes focused on the dusty chinks of grey light coming from around the edge of the curtains. He ran his tongue along the fuzz on his teeth and licked the top of his lip which was still covered in sweet sticky sambuca.

He stumbled to the bathroom to get a glass of water, there were no pint glasses only a tiny little tumbler – 'Fuck it, it will have to do.' The thimble-sized glass of water did little to quench his thirst – it felt rather like the first trickles of the rainy season forming a tiny waterhole in a desert, where five thousand small insects and a water buffalo are supposed to rehydrate after months of drought.

He went back to bed. Sleep was the only thing that could cure the gross pounding in his head. He lay down relieved to be prostrate.

DONG... DONG... DONG... DONG... DONG... DONG... DONG... DONG... DONG... DONG... 'That fucking bell', he thought. It was 8.50. DONG... DONG... DONG... DONG... Not even on the hour. DONG... DONG... DONG... DONG... Slightly warped, hardly sanctifying. DONG... DONG... DONG... DONG... It carried on.

It was like some kind of retribution, he thought, for the life he was living. DONG... DONG... DONG... DONG... DONG... He should have joined the building apprentice scheme on the Olympic building site, rather than stick at the job he hated, selling telephone systems to offices in a recession. He should have done a lot of things. He should have taken the book back to the library. DONG... DONG... DONG... DONG... DONG... He should not have let his drinking drive Sarah away. The night that he had hit her through drunken fury was the last that he had seen or heard of her and that had been eight months ago.

He should have not stayed at Zulus drinking until the end, swaying and shouting through the incongruous company of Afrikaners, students, Poles and east Londoners. He should not have been there in the first place. He had gone after work, as usual on the pretext that he would have one pint. Andre, the Afrikaner had insisted that they spend their hard-earned paltry pounds on a crappy South African beer. Being the only drinking establishment in Leytonstone that he ever drank in, Adam the Pole and him had agreed. He was also terrified of Andre, his thick-necked opinion on everything, the stories of murders and guns and rapes in the country that he had left.

There was no-one in there when they walked in, ordered their crappy South African beers and sat at the splintered bench in the beer garden. The volleyball court, which now resembled a giant sand ash tray, was being swept by a bar worker in an attempt to improve the surroundings. It had started with beer, then there was the cheap Saffa brandy, the drink probably responsible for stripping Andre of his brain cells. DONG... oh no then there was the tequila, DONG... sambuca, DONG... – a healthy dab of drone which he had never taken before, DONG... DONG... DONG... and then dancing and shouting and Andre fighting. Amy, DONG... . He remembered talking to her – a slurred, spitty, sweaty encounter which had left her trapped quivering in the corner squashed with nowhere to go except to listen to his intoxicated moaning about the fucking bell that never stops ringing and how he should have worked on the Olympic site and was it not fantastic that there was an opportunity like that just around the corner. He had also rambled about the bell and the fact that it was haunting his waking, sleeping and especially the hours in between.

'Perhaps,' she had ventured, 'you need something else in your life apart from this.' He looked around him. He was having a whale of a time; he loved it here, the soft rock, followed by shite R&B. Andre bumping his way across the dance floor followed by a dozen pairs of murderous eyes, as he groped any arse he could feel on the way.

What more could he possibly want? It was Friday night, work for the week was finished, he did not have to talk to his colleagues or anyone on the phone for a whole two days. Life was great.

Except, DONG... it wasn't. He was now lying alone in bed listening to god's wrath in the form of church bells punishing him for his debauchery, DONG... his unfulfilled potential. He peered out the curtain, it was grey outside, no one was going to the church, in his two years of living on that road, in its shadow, he had never seen anyone enter the church, not even on a Sunday. Another day spent in shivering self hatred with nothing to do except wait for the bell to stop, DONG... DONG... DONG...

Beyond the spire, he could see the cranes on the Olympic site. He could see the outside edge of the shell of the main stadium taking impressive shape. Everyone who lived in the adjoining boroughs had a right to training and to work there and he had been all set to go along to an induction on how to get a job. He had not made it because he had been up until five in the morning doing angel dust and then straight to the pub at 11.30 to carry on the bender. DONG...

What else had Amy said? He thought to himself. He should go to yoga, it would help him clear his mind and focus on what he wanted, some bollocks about balance. It would turn his alcohol-racked body into a well-honed example of masculinity. He looked at the crumpled leaflet in his pocket she had given him: 'Kundalini Yoga at the 491 Project'. He knew where that was, it was a commune near the station run by like-minded free spirits. He had thought it was an art gallery, maybe he would go.

'Breathe in through your nose and out through your mouth and then breathe from your stomach – huh huh huh,' chanted the yoga instructor. She had dreadlocks, tattoos and three rings in her nose, homage to the lifestyle she had chosen to lead. Her body was taut through her practice and her expert stomach breathing left him feeling inadequate, uneasy and nauseous. The chant at the beginning was eerily cult-like. 'And cobra.' He looked around; the room was filled with a group of people who looked like they did yoga, stringy and sinewy. The only two other men looked particularly yoga-like with shaved heads, veins lining their foreheads and tapestry trousers. He, on the other hand, was not built for flexibility, a six-foot Welshman, with a beer belly from life's excesses that made it hard for him to touch his toes gracefully. The physical effort was making his red face even more flushed and the five pints he had drunk last night were seeping through his skin, covering him with a slimy layer of very hopsy, pungent sweat.

He could see Amy at the back, concentrating on lifting her chest to the ceiling, looking serenely ahead. He hung his head forward and stared at the collected dust on the ground. It had gathered on the parquet flooring, heaping into the corners in little mounds. He could see the hairs on the back of the leg of the girl in front of her and the slightly dimpled skin where her shorts had ridden up. The smell of the dust mingled with the smell of sweaty gym clothes and farts.

His mind wandered to the Olympic site just down the road. In two years' time primed athletes would be searching for glory in the stadium that would dominate the east London skyline. He had walked past it on the way to yoga and wondered what it would be like to be involved with something that would bring so much change to the area. He could see the sturdy mesh of the entrance archway taking shape and the fluid curves of the velodrome. The wall protecting the site had sprung up quickly, cordoning off the world of cranes, tractors and mud from the commuters, mothers and school children, Ghanaian chop shop owners, Nigerian taxi drivers and Pakistani mosque goers, all going about their everyday lives. It had felt like an American military operation in a film about discovering alien life. He had expected to see some official looking men in big white suits bouncing around. Inside the walls there were machines with wheels as big as houses toiling away constructing, building and bulging with activity. Outside the barricades, the streets of Leytonstone and Stratford hummed with normality.

'And feel your spine stretch,' she was gripping his shoulders pulling them back and telling him to lengthen his spine. Kundalini yoga apparently translated into a snake coiled at the bottom of the spine; he felt like he had a snake at the front as well. The flow of blood from moving around in the peculiar, carnal yoga positions had made him feel a bit more virile and alive. He still had a splitting headache though.

After the session, while people gathered around to talk about yoga stuff, he sipped his bottle of water, feeling like a bit of a professional and wiped some sweat off his brow with a spare pair of socks. 'Did you only tell me about the bell because I am religious,' she asked inquisitively. He stifled a nervous giggle and mumbled something about how he had been drunk and talking nonsense. He had forgotten what he had told her about the church bell when they had met on Friday night.

'Would you like a cup of tea?' She was putting the kettle on in the communal kitchen. 'There is usually an art exhibition in here, you should come sometime and have a look.' He was always saying that he should go to art galleries and museums or even a walk in Epping Forest but he never did, as he was usually too sick from the excesses of alcohol and drugs, feeling too anxious to leave the house and venture out and interact with other people.

They left yoga and while they walked, Amy talked about her work and how she had to fill in numerous forms in order to gain access to a child who had been beaten. She also moaned but how the budgets had been cut, putting more pressure on her and her colleagues.

She was ok, Amy, a bit of a hippy but ok. He had met her in the Sheepwalk where he went to watch a friend in a band. Sarah had just left him and he had been on a three day drinking binge which led to him falling him over and cracking his head open on the bar, before being booted out onto the street. He could not even remember if the band was any good. She had been handing out flyers for his friend to get some extra money and looked after him as he crumpled on the pavement.

He had heard that she had left Belfast after all her family, bar her brother, were killed when their house had burnt down. She had travelled to India where she immersed herself in the tripped out haze of Anjuna. When her boyfriend overdosed on everything she worked in a nunnery, sleeping in a bed with a crucifix above it, ensuring that any sleepless night was spent staring up at the suffering Jesus Christ. It had made her think about things and she came to London and studied social work and was now a Catholic, hippy, social worker who was drunkenly accosted by him whenever they bumped into each other. She had patched up his head that night on the pavement and had helped patch up his heart after Sarah had left.

He always felt bad when he moaned about his life and slightly stupid when he explained to her that the bell from the church next to his house haunted him as it droned on and on. He looked at her walking along, clutching her yoga mat. 'Why are you being so nice to me?' he asked. She looked at him, 'Everyone needs to be helped out occasionally, sometimes people get stuck and they need a push in a new direction or just someone to listen to them. I have had people do the same for me when I've been in a bad way. I am just doing that for you – karma, if you like.'

She was standing in front of the North by North West mural in the passageway of Leytonstone station. 'How apt,' he said. 'Why?' Amy inquired, turning to take it in. The mosaic mural was one of the seventeen that line the damp concrete of the station with colour and culture. 'The title is apparently taken from Hamlet, - I am but mad north-northwest: when the wind is southerly I know a hawk from a handsaw.' He was sure that Hamlet would have related to the ringing of the church bell as a symptom of madness. 'I didn't take you for a Shakespeare fan,' she smiled. She had never noticed the murals before and walked along saying their names out loud. 'Well there you go, you have taught me something, it's not all me helping you after all.'

They emerged the other side of the tube station and walked past the Polish supermarket, the Vietnamese nail place and Percy Ingles bakery, where they bought an iced bun each to eat on the bench outside the church by the crossroads. He felt better, more positive, maybe Amy was right, he just needed a push in the right direction. She finished her bun and gathered up her bag. They had an awkward moment where he did not know whether to kiss her good bye or not and they kind of hovered in a limbo. 'I will see you on Wednesday,' she said, 'make sure you come, else the full benefits are not really felt.' He smiled and agreed that he would definitely be there on Wednesday.

He felt good as he walked down the road, he had done some exercise and the sun had started to peak through the grey clouds. He turned the corner towards home with a spring in his step. 'Howzit bru!' He heard someone shout down the street. He emerged from his bubble, he knew only one person that would greet him in that way. Andre was walking down the other side of the street, overalls dirty with paint and dust. It was too late to avoid him. Heart sinking, he smiled and waved. 'Coming for a pint?' Andre asked. They were nearly at Zulus and before he could think about his answer, he was in there with a pint of that South African beer and a whiskey chaser. Andre had laughed when he heard that he had been at yoga. 'What you want to do that hippy crap for?' Telling him the truth would be pointless. Instead he bought another round of tequilas and explained that yoga is sometimes worth going to because you can look at the women's arses. Andre's eyes lit up at this and he said he might look into it. The thought of Andre at the yoga class in an art gallery down the road made him chuckle a little as the warm glow of alcohol took over his body and senses. He couldn't imagine a 22-stone prop forward pulling off some of those positions.

The sound of his alarm clock mixed with the DONG... DONG... DONG... of the church bell. He groaned and stretched his leg out which felt odd, he was still wearing his tracksuit bottoms from yoga but he could feel something else. DONG... DONG... DONG... He felt like crying, he felt like his brain had been pierced with a thousand knives. He lifted his hand to his face and felt the crusting of blood DONG... He moved his hand around his eye, it felt swollen. He realised that it was not that he did not want to open his eye, but he couldn't. DONG... Flashes from the night before started to come back to him with brutal clarity; he felt the panic tighten his chest. DONG... They had seen one of the sinewy yoga men from the class and started on him. Andre liked fighting and he was too far gone to have cared. The yoga man chose to launch himself at him with a punch to the eye DONG... he remembered falling to his knees, DONG... the right one onto a shot glass which shattered and had no doubt left a bloody cut. The excavation drill was in his head again, the bell was haunting him and he needed to go to hospital for stitches.

DONG... DONG... DONG... DONG... DONG... DONG... DONG... DONG... DONG... the bell rang, he counted the chimes. He thought if he counted them, it would stop the panic attack that was about to engulf him. He couldn't breathe. Nine he thought to himself. He looked at his phone, the clock read 9am. The bells were ringing right. He bolted upright in bed and hauled his leg over the side. He could see a dark patch of congealed blood on his knee. He looked in the mirror by the bed, his left eye was swollen shut and there was a cut on the eyelid with a big crust of dark blood making it impossible to open. His jaw was black from the impact and he could not really move his neck. His head felt like it was full of concrete and cotton wool at the same time. His heart raced as he stifled a sob of self pity and peered out the curtain, terrified at the prospect of the outside world. The church loomed back at him. He had to call Marie at work to say he would not be coming in. With shaking hands, he dialed the number. 'This is your fourth sick day in six weeks and your second formal warning,' said a detached voice at the end of the line, 'you are in deep trouble.'

He didn't know whether he cared or not, he was in too much pain. He sank back onto his pillows, his whole body trembling as his world caved in. He lay there unable to move. DONG... DONG... DONG... DONG... DONG... DONG... DONG... DONG... DONG... DONG... 10am. He knew they would be right again somehow. He lay there all day listening on the hour to the church bell and they rang on the hour at the correct time all day. He watched the light and shadows of the day pass behind the curtains, only knowing what time it was because of the bell.

It was dark by the time he got up. He limped up the street and onto the bus. Everyone was staring at him. He avoided eye contact as the bus lurched towards Whipps Cross. When he did look up, while they were stopped at a set of red lights, he saw Amy waiting to cross. She saw him and waved but then saw his eye and dropped her hand, a look of disappointment crossed her face. He didn't think he would be making yoga tomorrow. He hung his head and the bus carried on.

***

DONG... DONG... DONG... DONG... DONG... DONG... DONG... DONG... he woke up, his injuries aching. Eight a.m, he thought as he hoisted his injured leg over the bed and gingerly lifted his hea. He had things to do. He walked out of the front door, past the church, staring up at the spire. The sun broke behind it, hurting his swollen eye. The sky was blue as he opened the door to the internet café. He sat down in front of the computer and typed into the search engine: Working for London 2012, National Skills Academy for Construction.

He would not be walking home past Zulus again.

ENFIELD

Nne, biko

Nne, biko

Uchenna Izundu

I

The air was seasoned with buzzing laughter and chatter about homework, feisty teachers, fit bodies and strict parents. Bursts of colour entered Ndi's peripheral vision as teenagers ran for buses that swung into Edmonton Green bus station. Strewn between the groups laden with Asda and Tesco bags, buggies, weight and faith that things could only get better were the harassed mothers, shuffling pensioners, yo-yo dieters and upbeat immigrants desperate for work.

They were all on the hustle; Ndi was sick of signing on in the dreary magnolia JobCentre Plus office on Fore Street where its sewage drains perfumed the air one fortnight or his advisor suffered from banging breath the next. He flared at their patronising tones in threatening his pitiful allowance. He tensed at the crap compulsory literacy and numeracy tests for job searching training that still wasn't bringing no dough, man. Miserable motherfuckers: the routine was soulless. Read the scribbles in his JSA diary, sign a line, click a mouse and get out. They thrived on ticking boxes, suffocating bureaucracy and massaging government stats in the poor part of Enfield where over 60 per cent of its residents survived on benefits and Sky.

Using his antiseptic tissues to wipe the greasy job listings screens, Ndi shuddered at the parade of young and old, fat and thin, light and dark, thick and smart, bent and straight men and women crippled by the disease of frustration. The advisors couldn't inspire them with boasts of the area's work ethic in the last century with furniture making and timber transportation by barge along the River Lee Navigation. They didn't know; fudge it. There were no jobs now, innit?

Security at the JobCentre knew Ndi for trying to save the startled plump Asian advisor from a clawing client. They bullocked him for it. Ndi was shocked: he went home with a thumping headache and bruised arms that ached for days – determined that if that shit ever happened again he would knock *them* out.

Each time Ndi left the JobCentre, he wondered where was his *chi*? Was his god sleeping? He began to bind, cast, and laminate all enemies of progress, calling on God to give him a J, O, damn B with prospects. The answer was always the same: overdose on McDonald's or KFC, which were next door. These outlets, mobile phone kiosks and bric-a-brac shops vied for attention on the long, bedraggled, grey street, punctuated with the occasional green tree and sparkling hubs of Turkish, Asian and African enterprise. Ndi Snr, a short and stocky mini cab driver, was unsympathetic. 'Eh-heh, you see what happens when you don't want to read!' Whether awake or asleep, whenever he tossed and turned, his father's voice pricked him all over like feasting chinchi.

And the memories were so hard to drown; they kept thrashing to the surface.

His screaming disappointment when Ndi dropped out of college 'coz it's hard, innit!' Pulling on his ear, Ndi Snr bellowed, '*Gee nti,* what hard are you talking? Did you carry water from the stream? Read by candle when Nepa took light? Look for food during Biafra? That spirit of stubbornness that is blocking you from getting your certificates should leave you today, today!'

Ndi's vision changed; he stopped looking up and started looking down as he flirted with one low paid job and another – cleaner, painter/

decorator, security. None lasted more than six months; he either quit, was fired, or laid off.

Nne, his buddy-buddy, remained constant; they were always burning credit blowing 'tory. Consolation, encouragement, and cussing the hell out of their situations. She was multitasking: her access course into teaching, working part-time in the West End, and her mother's wahala about housework and rent contributions.

His relationship with Nne was sealed at primary school until she returned home at the age of 10 when her father remarried. Once a year they could gist on and on till the break of dawn during family visits in the summer holidays. Their motto became, *'if you do me, I do you'.*

So, he graduated to his first run-in with the police around Tottenham posing in his friend's stolen car. 'Did I raise a thief? Why are you allowing the devil to operate in you?' Ndi Snr yelled.

He manned up into a 419 sideline when Adeyemi became pregnant at nineteen. There was stunned silence when the Ibo grapevine grassed him up on the £5000 scam he had jiggery-pokeried on no-one of someone that one other person knew. 'Ndubuisi, you mean you've grown wings like dis?' Ndi Snr screeched as his fists connected with his son's jaw. 'You're now congratulating yourself, abi?' When the baby was stillborn, his father said it was a relief that Ndi had escaped his responsibilities. That catapulted his exit from the crummy two bedroom council flat they had shared in Upper Edmonton since ma's passing from sickle cell anaemia.

II

'Come again?'

Nne jerked forward in her seat; Mrs Briscoe bristled. 'I know it's not what you want to hear but...'

'But it's complete shit!'

Mrs Briscoe flushed a faint red that surprisingly added some delicacy to her stern features and Nne immediately apologised. Her thoughts fluctuated between jealousing the angular frame of her boss who had birthed five children and internally cussing the day she first picked up chalk to write equations in this difficult secondary school. The irony of the situation was not lost on Nne at all. Here she was sitting in the headteacher's office facing a potential disciplinary for a wayo-no-good-waste-of-a-lyin'-wor-wor pupil who actually thought she was too damn nice.

What kind wahala be dis one, now? Can you imagine? Nne thought. *Kai, this country is going to the dogs!*

She tried desperately to match Mrs Briscoe's cool, calm composure. 'I don't understand how Grace can even have the audacity to challenge this decision.'

'If it's any comfort, I'm amazed at how aggressive Grace's parents have become about this issue. They're all saying you assaulted her. We have a duty to consider their claims.'

'But she was cheating! I saw her!'

Mrs Briscoe held her steely stare and handed a sheaf of papers over with guidelines on how the investigation would be handled.

She knew that Nne's response – of dragging the screaming pupil out of the exam hall – was the diluted version: if permissible, Nne would have slapped Grace. How could she respond to this hunched firecracker with long black locs? She was just so, well, *raw* with her gold nose stud gleaming on flawless Oreo-coloured skin. This was a farcical situation: Grace was pleading ignorance to cheating in an exam as Nne, the invigilator, hadn't stated that this was forbidden. And now her parents were making a dreadful fuss that she had to manage.

Mrs Briscoe smoothed back her coiffed grey bob.

'That will be all, Nne.'

***

Pausing outside of the staffroom, Nne's ears were sprinkled with muffled giggles. She tutted and battled the burning tears. Six years of self-improvement investment was on the verge of just melting like that? All that hypertension in reading for her teaching exams? All these early starts and late nights? She now needed glasses as she was squinting from marking students' papers. *For what now, for what? Ah-ah!*

She snapped her fingers. God forbid! She had J.E.S.U.S; it was time for fasting and praying. This disciplinary would not succeed.

She swung open the door and was instantly irritated by her milky-way colleagues sprawled on sofas sipping tea and coffee and eating custard creams, who massacred her name to 'Innay' because they refused to hear Igbo. They were armed with mummy, daddy, equities, and trust funds.

She had no one to call upon to bail her out of this spiralling shit. Nne had fled Lagos with £200 in her pocket at the age of 17. When Popsie remarried, Nne was convinced that her stepmother had jazzed him. She was no longer his sweetheart and was bewildered by this snappy man who had abandoned Momsie in London.

It was Ndi that she belled regularly to lament about her stepmother's increasing wickedness as the years progressed. 'Ndubuisi biko, help me to leave now!'

He tracked Momsie when Nne first landed in town. Until tomorrow he had never quite understood how she escaped, especially as Nne had said that her British passport was locked up in the family home in Aba in the east. She just shrugged: 'I forged another in Oluwole – anything is for sale there, even human heads.'

The pupils' babbling in the hallway jolted Nne into the present.

This shitty day needed to be erased with a spliff: that drag would pacify her. In her head, she could already hear Ndi moaning about it. Nne took a deep breath as she packed her belongings: her tart response to his lectures still remained the same – drug use is different to drug abuse.

III

Ndi was tired of scavenging in the 99p stores in the rusty and crusty concrete jungle shopping mall in Edmonton Green, which spat out empty units from a biting recession.

Crashing at Momsie's place over the past few months left him distinctly uncomfortable. She was clocking all shifts going to save money for a brief 'holiday' at home. He was bumming around.

Nne had become increasingly aloof: she had an outside life that he couldn't relate to. This course, that concept; this assignment, that lecturer, Mr Clever Clogs, Miss Thicko. She came back late; she was tired. She couldn't talk. She didn't listen any more. And she was impatient with his vagueness about what he wanted to do with his life. She always seemed distracted by school – it was all she bloody well talked about. He could no longer confide in her as she was hell bent on cracking teaching to escape the tiny meandering roads, boxy cottages, and high-rise flats of Edmonton.

Momsie listened though: she squeezed his hand, patted his back, teased him about his wide feet. She always asked if he'd eaten and urged him to reconcile with his father and when he broke down Ndi knew he was starved of tenderness and her smoked chicken jolloff rice. She drilled him on what his plans were and was vexed by 'I dunno; I'm seein' how it goes, innit?' So, when the bulbs popped, Ndi handled it. When the garden needed mowing, he sorted it. He made pepper and okasi soups, Momsie's favourites. He painted the house – desperately aware that he needed to earn his keep.

And that's how it hit him one Tuesday afternoon whilst washing goat meat to roast in the oven. He heard the door flap shut and picked up a leaflet about a talk in Ponders End community centre the following week by local entrepreneurs. If no-one was going to employ him, he needed to employ himself. Pennies needed to become pounds ASAP.

What business could he do? He frowned: whatever it was it needed to be recession proof. Then, as he began seasoning the meat, it occurred to him that people would always need to eat. Why couldn't he cook for them? Naijas were always shakin' a tail feather.

Ndi researched the internet to collect some ideas. When his funding applications failed Momsie sponsored the business. Ndi tensed at the offer but remembered his father's reprimands whenever he rebuffed help: a man who believes that he can do everything should dig a grave and bury himself!

Ndi found the monthly networking evenings empowering as he learnt about finance, marketing, and legal issues. With other entrepreneurs struggling he was no longer the fuck ups specialist. When he saw his first grand sitting in his business account, Ndi was dazed. That changed to elation; he bought himself a nice suit on sale from Burton. From there the business grew: one order became two. Ten became twenty. His customers' recommendations were sweet: he was booked out for the next six months. Nne teased him about his *chi*'s awakening and promised to accompany him to one of these forums on South Street, nibbling soggy cheese sandwiches and swallowing flat coke.

That's why he was waiting for her at Edmonton Green bus station. Was this the first time she was late? Hell to the damn no.

When he saw the bulging Primani carrier bag in her hand, Ndi really became agitated.

He bit his lip and clenched his fists wondering how he was gonna put her on lockdown with security officers in lime green vests darting into war formations whenever trouble zipped and zapped amongst yout' dem.

Na wa, o.

As usual, she looked on point in dark blue treggings that defined thighs delectable for suya, nyash, and an itsy-bitsy waist topped off with snakeskin knee high stiletto boots: an antidote to her 'smallie' complex.

Ndi was amazed that she could function in them and rock her locs despite the lamentations from her aunts, uncles, cousins and anyone else that played stickybeak in her business. When she was on the damn mobile, it was raucous laughter lathered in sticky, spicy gossip.

Yet he was dry like harmattan: cruising in his double bedroom that groaned under his stuff. His mates rarely persuaded him to step out, down beer, shake waist, and enjoy. Chy, how times had changed.

He signalled her to come quick now – mek dey do. Nne caught his eye, saw he was boning, and ended the conversation.

'Ah beg o, mek you no vex,' she whispered hugging him. 'Cool down.'

Ndi pointed at the Primani bag. 'I know, yeah, you came straight from work and it ain't work stuff in dere. Why are you goin' to Primark when you *know* you're meant to be meetin' me? I don't get you, really I don't.'

'Ah-ah, is that all?' She beamed at him and pulled out her oyster as they entered the packed bus. 'Nna, this is therapy. Can you believe I just found out that Paul has girlfriend?'

Ndi laughed – Paul was her FWB. 'Really, how did dat happen?'

'Helen just called me to find out how we're gonna do the kids' assembly later this weekend and she mentioned dat Paul's girlfriend is doing barbie. 'Do I wanna come?' I said: 'Eh? Which kind girlfriend?' She said dat her and Paul have been dating now for the past six months – didn't I know?' Nne blew a bubble and popped it. 'Heh, I just called this bwoy now two's two's and do you know what he's tellin' me?'

'What?'

'Since when did he become accountable to me? Aren't we both grown adults? They haven't agreed anything between themselves, o: him and dis chick aren't in a relationship.'

Ndi snickered.

'I don't know why you think that's funny, bro. I went mad! I said you was fucking well accountable when I was chokin' dat monkey!'

Ndi winced at the kids around them. 'Nne, must you be so blaytant?'

'It's da fucking truth! Bastard, a *whole* me deputy girlfriend? For where? All dis shit for someone who get liver to wear white shoes? Eeh, I don't roll with mans that has gyal, o. If you wanna give me benefits, let's all know that we're single and ready to mingle. It's coz I have nothin' else beta to do than catch STDs, abi?'

Suck teeth.

'You have a weird logic, do you know that?'

Her response was her fiercest cut eye.

'I'm more pissed that I went through three cigarettes after bullocking him on the phone and I know when I go home,' Nne's voice dropped to a whisper, 'I'm gonna need a spliff.' She stretched in her seat. 'That's why I had to reach into Primark; dis stuff was on sale so even beta!'

Nne appraised him in the navy jacket that sculpted his slim shoulders, crisp white shirt, and matching trousers. Bobo! What a dramatic change to his tired skinny jeans, trainers and hoodies. His goatee was cut low and she noticed confidence in his light brown eyes that hadn't existed before. 'Fine boy, no craw craw. You're lookin' sharp; I like it.'

He shrugged. 'Business is good.'

'I can tell! How many food orders have you got now?'

Ndi smiled shyly and sat up straighter. 'It's coming up to forty – about seven grand worth of business.'

'So you'll be able to pay back Momsie then?'

He bowed his head. 'She said no pressure, it's all good.'

'I'm glad she hooked you up – she's always liked you. Ndubuisi, Ndubuisi!' she laughed touching up her lip gloss. 'At last she's off my case and is now harassing you. E no easy o.'

'For real. Anyways, I wanna take you out to dinner to celebrate my first five grand,' he said depressing the bell to stop the bus. 'Mek we enjoy! I'm also renting a new place to myself in Winchmore Hill!' He chuckled.

'I can't wait to leave shank town I'm tellin' you. Mans always has to sleep with one eye open these days, y'get me?'

Jealousy strangled her into widening her eyes and gaping. Why him? He'd only been self employed for six months and yet was sprinting over Great Cambridge Road into serene suburbia with classy restaurants, clean wide streets, imposing properties, and grandiose pubs. Who was his *chi* in this business? Was hers sleeping? Didn't she attend uni? For eighteen months as a teacher all she had to show was a £20,000 debt doused in blood, sweat and tears, and an investigation that had shaken her to the core. She was living in crowded accommodation where sullen housemates refused to respect the kitchen and neighbours dumped splitting mattresses and old clothes on street corners. People were so trifling; it was abracadabra with black recycling bins and foxes had the balls to bop beside residents at night.

He fed her as promised, but it was difficult to relax following her visit to his beautiful one bedroom Victorian flat with high ceilings, polished fireplaces, original caramel wooden floorboards and French patio doors that led to a charming white rose bush garden.

She couldn't touch the brand new furniture that he bought. She couldn't blow the big grammar he had these days from pushing his business. Ndi had an outside life that she couldn't relate to. This order, that business term; this obstacle, that government policy, Mr Supplier, Miss Recommendation. He came back late, was tired, and couldn't talk. And he dismissed her stories of wrestling a white middle class power structure where she had to work twice as hard just to keep up with 'Leave, innit?' That rankled her: there was an effing recession! He didn't *listen* anymore and was spraying the poppin' punani glitterati who prowled the clubs, restaurants, shops and bowling alleys.

IV

Walking briskly along Fore Street towards Momsie's place, Nne was eager to reduce the bloated belly from choppin' welu welu at Helen's flat. The girl had thrown down a serious feast shah to secure the crown in their *Come Chop With Me* spinoff.

Ndi had laughed off joining them claiming unfair advantage as he was running a catering business. His rejection stung and Nne just couldn't understand her reaction to him. Was she hatin'? Nne wondered. A *whole* me asking who dey dere? His fair skin was shining; he was looking finer after gyming. The more he became a dick, the more she wanted him. When she joked about spending his money, he played hard to get. Wetin happen? Anyone else, she would have dumped long time. Haba! But Ndi...? She was hanging on, just about, and it frightened her being a groupie.

Before the locs era, Ndi was the only person she trusted to get down and dirty in removing her extensions – not even Momsie – so hair couldn't stew in any juju pot. After all, had this woman bothered to look for her in Naija? Pass on any message? Pray for Nne's deliverance when her stepmother lavished knocks on her head? Did Momsie weep at all at all for her only child?

Kai, it was cold! She nestled into the upturned coat collar as the chilling wind bit her neck. Only in this nonsense country in May would you still be rockin' and rollin' scarves and thermal wear because spring refused to comot. It was at times like this that Nne longed for Naija's sultry heat as she preferred sweating to shivering any day.

Spit whizzed past her; a middle aged man sauntered ahead oblivious to the screw face burning into his back. She didn't have the strength to challenge him. What was it with these animals masquerading as human beings? Another twenty minutes and she would be at Momsie's where she could chillax and pick up her forgotten books.

With sunlight streaming through the lacy nets, the tableaux bounced back the howls that fractured every crevice of the parlour.

Nne was the only one screaming.

Nne, biko: mother, please!

The stuffed silence wasn't enough – it wasn't enough because nothing was changing. The dinky grey pebble dashed terraced cottages on Cornwallis Grove were framed by drab brown curtains. The recycling boxes spewed crap onto the road and there was the faint rumble of the rubbish van progressing on its collection route. Bin bags piled like pimples ready to burst and opposite the house she could hear Amy's terrier yapping excitedly.

Nne saw Ndubuisi's *'chi'* in this business.

They stared back: Ndubuisi and Momsie – her chocolate nipple nestled in his mouth and his hands splayed on her naked nyash.

TOWER HAMLETS

The Djinn

The Djinn

Tabitha Potts

Salimah heard the front door slam. Ibrahim had left their house for his early morning shift. Reluctantly, she got out of her bed, shivering slightly as the house was never quite warm enough. Omar and Farihah were still asleep, so she had time to wash and say her dawn prayers before dealing with the children. Drawing back the curtain, she saw that the street light was still emitting its sickly glow, while the rest of the street was plunged in darkness. Over the wrought iron fence she could see the churchyard, the gravestones looming masses against the grass. Further away in the distance, Canary Wharf flickered, its sparkling lights adding a incongruously glamorous backdrop to Salimah's immediate surroundings of Victorian terraces, each small front garden signaling the socio-economic background of its inhabitants with unerring accuracy: here, an aspirant box tree in a square metal container, there a defiant multicoloured display of geraniums. Salimah's home said little about her. Even the lightbulbs hung on their flexes with no shades to shield their glare, but the house itself was scrupulously tidy, every surface reflecting back the light like a mirror.

She showered and dressed and then, went to pray. Intoning the familiar words, she felt her mind calm and become still and was half way through when a noise in the room startled her enough for her heart to pound uncomfortably for a few seconds. Eventually she discovered the source of the noise; the scroll inscribed with verses from the Qur'an that she had hung on the wall had fallen from its hook. Carefully hanging it back up, she made sure it was fastened firmly. A sound from the room the children shared made her go to them. Omar was still fast asleep, but Farihah was up in her cot, gripping the sides and staring at her mother with an intense, questioning gaze. Salimah picked her up, enjoying the feeling of the small, warm body wrapped in hers. She went downstairs with the little girl, leaving Omar to wake by himself and come down.

It was daylight by now and as Omar had not emerged Salimah left Farihah in her highchair for a moment and went upstairs to check on him. He woke up when she stroked his cheek but she noticed he felt a little hotter than usual to touch. She sighed. This could mean foregoing her trip to the market and Brick Lane. Standing by the door, while the three year old reluctantly got out of bed, she felt a sudden, icy chill. It was as though someone had opened a window directly behind her; the feeling was so strong she even looked around. Of course, there was nothing there. But she shivered and decided to put on her warmest veil rather than any of the lighter ones she sometimes wore.

A couple of hours later, she was wandering down Whitechapel Market with the two children safely stowed in their pram. Omar still was not his normal lively self and was napping, long eyelashes flat on his cheeks. Passing a stall of fruit and vegetables, jackfruit, okra and bunches of herbs, Salimah found herself transported for a moment back home as she inhaled the distinctive warm tang of coriander. She was in the kitchen, holding onto her mother's bright sari while her mother prepared supper, her hands stained with intricate patterns of henna as she chopped the herbs with expert speed. And then she was back on the windswept street where for a moment even the beloved faces of her children seemed unfamiliar, the faces of strangers, part of a life that might easily not have been hers.

Salimah was officially not the 'pretty one', that honour had belonged to Asna, whose luminous skin and whose eyes, large, limpid and richly fringed like the sleeping Omar's, had always seemed fit for a Bollywood star. Salimah's mother had whispered to her once: 'Someone will always watch over you, my darling'. But Asna married young and went to England, their mother died, and Salimah was left at home.

'Salamu Alaykum, what do you want today?' asked the stall holder in Bangla. Salimah bought two bunches of coriander and some chillis and hung the striped shopping bag over the handles of the pram. Omar woke up and started whining as he had spotted the ice cream shop next to Whitechapel station. Wearily, Salimah steered the pram away.

'1, 2. 1, 2. Bethnal Green? Anyone going to Bethnal Green? You got a bleeding heart, love? Is your heart bleeding?' came the disembodied voice of the office manager. White noise.

'Oh shut up.' Sheila on reception.

'76 I got something for you. Can you hear me 76?'

Ibrahim switched off the radio. He wasn't going to Bethnal Green, he was going home. The night had begun on Brick Lane with four noisy City boys wanting to be ferried from the curry house they were gracing with their presence to a strip joint in Hoxton. They had only tipped a pound, despite the fact that one of them had been sick in the back of the cab. The night continued with a drunken set of Rag Week students dressed as Alice in Wonderlands and Ronald McDonalds. One of the Ronalds was unable to remember where he lived, so Ibrahim had had to cross the Mile End Road three times. The scent of pine from the air freshener hanging in the front of the cab and the smell of vomit from the back seat mixed with the strident perfume of the Alices had made his head ache. As he didn't drink, the boredom of listening to the rambling chat from the back seat intensified his exhaustion – it was now 3.30am - but it was at last time to go home.

He found a spot for the cab outside the front door of the house. Meticulously tidy as always, he took his cleaning kit out of the back of the cab to replenish the air fresheners and tissues. He was startled to see

Salimah sitting at the kitchen table in her nightgown and overcoat. All the lights were on.

'Salamu Alaykum. What's wrong?'

'It's happened again.'

Ibrahim sighed.

'What's happened this time?'

Under the harsh lighting the whites of her eyes looked sore and her mouth looked pinched. The photograph of their wedding day back in the village was still on display on the windowsill. Salimah was dressed in her red and gold wedding sari, her usually solemn face smiling up at him. This morning she seemed very different to that young girl, yet it had only been four years since he had married her and brought her here.

'I cleaned the kitchen and then I was making some chicken – the one you like with spinach – while the children were taking their nap. I had my back to the storage cupboards and I was quite busy, you know, chopping up the onions. Then suddenly there was this loud noise, the doors of two of the cupboards opened behind me and everything fell out, the flour and the chickpeas landed on the floor and made it all dirty again. And I feel cold. I've been feeling cold all day.'

Her hands were wrapped up inside the overcoat .

Ibrahim went over to the cupboards and examined the shelves. She had tidied up but he could imagine an explosion of flour and mess. Nothing seemed to be near the edge of the shelves, and everything was safely in its box or packet. He looked under the stairs for his tools and checked the shelves with a spirit level, as he had done before. No, the shelves were not crooked in anyway. The units were cheap but fairly new. He shook his head.

'I can't see anything wrong. Are you sure you hadn't left something on the edge?'

'I'm sure!'

She was close to tears, he could hear it in her voice. He shivered. All this superstition was getting to him. He didn't need this, he wanted to sleep.

'I only feel peace when I am in the garden.'

Salimah's garden at the back of the house looked bleak now but in summer it would be bright with tier upon tier of chillis, squash and spinach, tomatoes and beans trained up canes and trellis. She had learned how to handle the sticky and dense London soil and grow the plants she remembered from home. The children and the garden were what made her happy, he thought, and felt another wave of irritation.

Asna offered Salimah another samosa but Salimah shook her head.

'*Acha*. You're looking too thin.'

'I can't eat much. I feel ill all the time. The only time I feel better is if I stay away from the house'.

Asna looked across the room at the children playing. She was proud of the lounge; she had had it decorated in a pale pink and it looked out onto a well-kept patio garden. Her eldest boy was showing Omar his toy collection, while Farihah was playing with the tea-set that Asna had got out for her. Her teenage daughter was too grown up for it now.

'Have you been to see the doctor?'

'I tell him about the chills I've been getting but he can't find anything wrong with me. He says I'm depressed and wants to give me pills.'

'You don't think... he could be right?'

'You've felt it. When you came round the other day you said you could feel how cold it was downstairs. And then you lost your purse.'

'I'm always losing it!'

'You said you'd put it in the kitchen, and it wasn't there. Why would you have left it in the bedroom? You didn't go in there.'

'The kids must have moved it.'

'I know there's something going on. I can feel it.'

'What did the Imam say?'

'He said some holy verses to make it go away. But it isn't gone. You know why I think that is?'

'You tell me.'

'It's something to do with that graveyard. I went to the council and asked us if they could help us find somewhere different to live, but it's going to take a long time'.

Asna watched Salimah, who was slumped in her armchair and staring at the floor. It was difficult; they had spent so long apart. She had left as a seventeen-year-old bride when her sister was just eleven. So many years when they could only talk on the telephone, miles apart, when they could have been together. Not enough visits back home, not enough to assuage the ache of missing her mother, not enough to keep her going through the grief after her mother died. Asna was proud of her marriage and her husband who now ran three successful shops, her stylish house and her kids. Her eldest daughter was at secondary school now and doing really well, and her boy was good at maths like his father. She wanted the same things for her sister.

'What does Ibrahim say?'

'Oh, he's working every night, I hardly see him and he's so tired. I think he is angry with me'.

The Curate was busy putting his notes together to prepare for the latest local history walk he was leading that Saturday. He loved to explore architecture, the traces of life lived hundreds of years ago that still survived unacknowledged in the modern chaos of the city. He loved the city farm, with its collection of hardy-looking Gloucester Old Spots, and went there often to visit the ruins of a mediaeval monastery that sat there unnoticed and unvisited except by a herd of athletic miniature goats. He would personally scrub away sprayed-on tags proclaiming the might and dominance of the Stepney Massive, or the same sort of graffiti he remembered from his own school days in Surrey, differing only in the types of names and the breadth of knowledge and inventiveness of the sexual techniques described, when they appeared on the walls of his beautiful church. He felt a thrill of pleasure when he looked around the stone building that sheltered his flock as it had done for centuries, withstanding even the Blitz. It had been a bit of luck to get a challenging, inner city parish, that had a church at its centre as old and beautiful as this. The Curate knew God didn't care about architecture, but was honest enough to admit to himself that he did.

The Curate's latest walk would start on Cable Street. He would explore the Ratcliffe Highway, where sailors from all over the world could once buy wild beasts of all descriptions, from lions and hyaenas to parakeets, moving on to the boundary stone marking the borough of Ratcliffe or 'Sailortown' notorious for its taverns, drug dens, brothels and general debauchery for hundreds of years. He would show them Stepney Causeway, where Dr Barnardo asked that one of the doors be kept permanently open after one child came looking for shelter, was turned away and died two days later of starvation on the streets. He thought how a historical distance could make a world where anything or anyone could be bought and sold and life itself was cheap seem exotic and fascinating while in fact the reality must have been – and was still – terrifying.

The Rector approached him as he was rearranging his notes.

'I have something interesting for you, Andrew,' he said cheerily. 'An infestation, you might say.'

'An infestation?'

Andrew, a serious man, had never understood the Rector's donnish mixture of learning and levity.

'A supernatural infestation. A young lady who lives in one of the old houses over there.'

He gestured towards the row of Victorian terraces opposite the graveyard.

'She has what appears to be a djinn problem. They're more common than you might imagine.'

'A djinn?'

'It's the same as the word for a genie, but it's not really a case of Scheherazade Aladdin, rubbing the lamp and three wishes. This is something more complicated, like a spirit that can do good or evil. She believes it is a Christian djinn, or ghost, or whatever you want to call it. You can come with me when we go to see her.'

'Isn't this more likely to be a case of something psychological?'

The Rector sighed.

'Of course that's something to consider. But in this case, if it will ease the anxiety of someone in our parish it is seen as worthwhile to say a few prayers of protection or peace, bless the house, that kind of thing. Deliverance, we call it. Besides, what is psychological, and what is not?'

'I don't follow you.'

'Non-believers would have us locate everything that does not fit into their scheme of things in the human imagination. "The sleep of reason produces monsters", as it says in the wonderful etching by Goya. But if you are willing to accept the possibility of an immortal, why not a monster, too? The Islamic belief is that djinns or genies are a separate part of creation, neither angels nor humans but beings created from fire and possessing free will, so capable of both good and evil. In the Judaeo-Christian tradition there are references to creatures similar to genies, too, the Mazikeen, who were children of Adam. These are centuries-old beliefs.'

'This confirms in me my belief that practical religion is a lot more straightforward than theoretical.'

The Rector smiled at him.

'Well, Andrew, in this case we'll be doing a little of both.'

At Salimah's house, the Rector introduced Andrew to the two women. Salimah had opened the door very swiftly, as though she had been watching out for them.

'My husband doesn't know you are coming here,' she said. 'He doesn't approve of all this, he thinks I am imagining things.'

She gestured vaguely, her hand taking in the small hallway and the stairs. They went to sit down in the front room, directly overlooking the graveyard.

'What will you do?' Asna asked.

'I will say a few words, in each room. I will be asking for a blessing, and protection, on the house and its inhabitants. You do not have to join in the prayers, but we will both give responses. You can remain silent, if you wish.'

The Rector smiled kindly at the two sisters, Asna in smart salwar kameez and a bright headscarf, Salimah more disheveled, as though the high standards of housekeeping apparent around them did not extend to her own appearance. He stood up and started speaking. There was no preamble, no book or candle. The Curate listened to the words and hoped that they would bring the listeners some reassurance.

'Visit, Lord, we pray, this place and drive far from it all the snares of the enemy.'

They continued from room to room, the small procession seeming overly large in the little house. The Curate admired the garden from the hallway window.

'Let your holy angels dwell here to keep us in peace, and may your blessing be upon it ever more; through Jesus Christ our Lord.'

It was in the children's upstairs bedroom that all of a sudden the Curate smelt it. It was a terrible stench, something with such an intensity of decay and horror in it that he almost gagged and rushed to the window.

'What is it?'

'You smell it, too?' asked Salimah.

'I can't smell a thing' said Asna. She was staring at him.

'It's horrible! Have you got mice, or rats? I've never...'

As he struggled with the old sash window, the smell disappeared.

'It's gone!'

Salimah shrugged. 'That's how it is, I smell it, my boy smells it. The little one, I don't know, but she wakes up at night sometimes screaming in her cot. My husband can't smell anything. I've done everything I can, I keep all the food hidden away, the council says there's no mice, there isn't anything'. She sounded weary rather than afraid.

The Curate noticed for the first time that there were cans of air freshener in every room.

The Rector looked at both the women. 'Excuse me. Shall we continue?'

Salimah was finding it hard to sleep after getting Farihah to settle down. She had tried taking the little girl into her own bed at first but it had not comforted her. None of the household had had much sleep for the last few nights and she had tried teething gel and painkillers in case that was what was causing the problem but it didn't seem to help. Farihah would be upright in her cot, shrieking and shrieking with real fear on her face.

'Night terrors,' Asna would tell Salimah on the phone.

But Salimah found that after one of these night-time episodes she would lie awake for what seemed like hours, staring at the cracks in the ceiling or watching shapes form and then disappear again in the patterns of the net curtains.

She heard Ibrahim's key turn in the lock. She knew his movements as well as her own. He went to the kitchen to put away his things and she heard him clattering about, opening and closing the cupboards. Then he came upstairs and went to the bathroom where she heard him washing. However, after that there was silence. Normally, at this point he would go to say his early morning prayers. Salimah got out of bed, wrapped a shawl around herself and went to look for him. The house was empty. She rang his mobile in panic.

'Where are you?' She told him what she had heard. He sounded sleepy.

'I'm coming home. I just finished my shift. Don't be silly, there's nothing to be afraid of.'

'It sounded as though someone else came into the house.'

'Well, no one did, you said the house was empty. Look, I'll be home soon, alright?' He cut off the call.

Ibrahim's presence once he was finally home in bed, his back turned to her and his eyes firmly closed, wasn't as reassuring as she had hoped.

Later, deep in sleep, Salimah awoke in confusion and terror with Ibrahim's hands fastened tightly around her neck. She wanted to cry out, but couldn't. It was like the worst sort of dream, but the pain and fear told her she was awake. Why were his hands so cold? His eyes were open but seemed glazed, not like those of the man she knew. The sense of something evil in the room was very strong now, so strong that Salimah could almost see it. His hands were tightening and Salimah was about to pass out, but she could see her mother's face flash brightly before her eyes. 'There will always be someone watching over you.' With a huge effort she managed to get her hands up to his and pulled at his fingers, pulling them back until his hands loosened their grip for a second, enough for her to pull her upper body from under his and then, kicking and scratching in terror, roll from the bed onto the floor. He got up and started walking towards her, his eyes still with that absent and terrifying stare.

Andrew found Salimah outside the church as he was locking up after the morning service. She was standing looking at the stained glass window. She smiled at him.

'It's beautiful. I've never really looked at it properly although I used to walk through the churchyard all the time.'

'How are you?'

'Much better. I wanted to come and say thank you for your help. I'm staying with Asna now, with my children.'

'And your husband?'

A shadow passed over her face. 'He has moved away from us now. He is living with his brother. I had to hit him with the bedside lamp, when the djinn took him over. I told the police he was sleepwalking because he'd been sleeping so badly. He didn't believe in the djinn, but it came to him.'

'I want to show you something. I only found this out recently, when I was researching for the history walk and came across a book about crime in the East End of London.'

He walked with her over to a grave that stood by itself at the edge of the churchyard. 'The occupant of this grave was originally intended to be a Mr Samuel Reed, a surgical instrument maker. He was a regular churchgoer and lived alone. He was discovered as a suicide in 1810 – he had hanged himself. A letter was found among his effects that confessed to the murder of a young woman ten years previously. The worst of this was that the body of his poor victim, a Miss Lizzy Barnes, who was identified by a locket he had kept among his papers, had been buried in his own home, under the floorboards.'

'Who was she?' asked Salimah, her eyes on the grave, where little could be seen except the name and the date, 1800. The inscription read simply 'May She Rest in Peace'.

'She was of uncertain occupation, and may have been what they called in those days a fallen woman, or a woman looking for work as a maid or housekeeper, it's hard to tell. He did not explain why he killed her in his letter, only spoke of "a need and compulsion so strong that it took hold of my mind, despite all efforts to tame it through prayer and good works. A need so strong that I almost fear it will outlive me." His confession asked that his victim be given a Christian burial in the plot that he had reserved for himself, where we are standing. He also asked forgiveness for his crime. His own body, as he was a self-confessed murderer and a suicide, was buried with a stake through his heart at a crossroad on Ratcliffe Highway'.

'Where did he live?' said Salimah, still looking at the gravestone.

The Curate pointed towards the row of Victorian terraced houses where Salimah's old house stood, now with metal shutters on the windows while the council found a new tenant.

'There.'

Salimah took a break after she had finished weeding the raised beds in the city farm and went to sit in the arbour she had created above the bench. All around her she could see the fruits of her work: squash whose ripe, plump flesh seemed to invite touching, bright chillis, plump aubergines with purple flesh, okra, spinach plants. All around her was beauty, calm and order. In the distance a cock crowed. Salimah herself was no longer thin and pinched, her skin glowed with health and her eyes shone. Sitting by herself in the garden, she thought: now I am home. Now I can live in peace.

HACKNEY

The Hackney Factor

The Hackney Factor

Ricky Oh

Eva hated how selfish people could be. Fucking hated it. And she didn't swear. Not out loud anyway. The other day, she was trying to get on a bus at Liverpool Street. She was there with a stuffed-to-the-gunnels bag full of nappies and wet wipes and spare trousers and juice and raisins and rice crispie-encrusted picture books and various plastic items in primary colours. But the hundreds of people, people without buggies or children or changing bags, didn't seem to see her. Everyone seemed to barge past her to get on. One person actually kicked Milly, her two-year-old, as she trampled over her buggy to swipe her Oyster while she barked into her Nokia. It was as if Eva and Milly and the buggy and the bags were invisible. But then she was SEP – somebody-else's problem – and, as such, pretty much something to be ignored.

When she did eventually get on – thank god there weren't any more people with buggies already on the bus, as she wouldn't have been allowed on at all – besuited business men tutted as she politely asked if they minded moving a little to let her into the designated space for buggies and prams. Then, when it felt like it couldn't get any worse, a middle-aged and slightly snotty-looking woman started holding onto the handles of the buggy for balance. Eva asked her, again politely, to let go as, if she fell over she would simply pull the buggy over with her and hurt her child, but the woman simply let lose a blast of abuse. Eva got off at the next stop and walked home.

But it wasn't all like that. In fact, it wasn't like that at all where she lived. And she was eternally grateful for that.

Okay, it had a bit of a bad reputation, murder mile everyone called it, but she had never seen anyone get shot. She had seen a car with police, do-not-cross tape around it and a bullet hole in its windscreen once, but that was all. No, Hackney was an ace place to live. And buses were brilliant, especially compared with trying to negotiate the Tube with a buggy and its associated paraphernalia. And the people who lived in Hackney were a pleasure to associate with.

The 'Hackney Factor' Eva called it. And it made her smile.

The nightmare journey was long forgotten now. Washed away by another day's duties and responsibilities. She had decided to take Milly to the library to get her her first library card. Which made her smile too as the new library in Hackney is on Reading Lane, a pun lost on Milly at the moment, but one Eva hoped to share with her daughter as soon as she might understand. She had handled the logistical nightmare of ferrying a small person around with aplomb today and the sun was shining and all was well with the world.

At the Millfields Road stop on Lower Clapton Road, Eva put the brake on the buggy and handed Milly a piece of banana. Milly dropped the fruit and pointed at the JCB that seemed to have been digging up the road for as long as she'd been alive. Today, instead of chug-chug-chugging at the macadam it sat empty and motionless as the blokes from the council or the gas board or electricity or Thames Water or whoever's turn it happened to be to cause traffic chaos in E8 today smoked rollies and laughed.

Behind her in the bus shelter old women sat down clutching their tartan wheelie trolleys for dear life and she smiled to herself some more as Milly stopped pointing at the digger, pointed at the old women and shouted 'twirly'. The word twirly was an anachronism from her childhood back in Nottinghamshire. Back then the old age pensioners' bus pass didn't allow anyone to travel before 9.30 in the morning and at 9.25 or so random old women and flat-capped old blokes would climb aboard the buses waving their passes asking in that peculiar north Nottinghamshire accent that still made Eva cringe a bit: 'Am a twirly to use me bus pass duck?' It still made her smile though.

As she and Milly waited for the 48 she couldn't help but think that no-one had called her 'duck' for a very long time. Even her mum, who had got the courage up to get the train from Nottingham down to St Pancras to visit her for a few days a couple of months back didn't use it any more. At the thought of her mum Eva stopped smiling and sighed a little sigh.

The long-awaited visit started out as a bit of a disaster actually. Eva had been telling her mum, now at a bit of a loose end after her dad had died the year before in a car accident, that Hackney was great and her new flat was ace and she should come down and see the sights and her granddaughter. Eva booked the tickets online and they had only cost a few quid, which Eva paid. Her mum got a lift to the station in Nottingham with someone from church and Eva had decided to get a taxi from St Pancras, to her flat. It was all sorted and it was going to be a lovely break for all three of them.

She had it all worked out. Her mum had a Freedom Pass thing so Eva had planned to get the bus to show her Clissold Park and Sutton House, to feed the ducks and have picnics and look at the rose gardens and sit by Regent's Canal, but it looked like it wasn't going to come off.

The problem was two-fold. First, her mum found the idea that she was entitled to free travel in the nation's capital simply too incredulous for words. In fact it took a whole day's persistent cajoling and convincing on Eva's part to get her to give it a go. ('Don't worry Mum I will have two pounds in my hand if the driver says it isn't valid' Eva explained, at which her mum nearly fainted at the idea that a bus journey anywhere could cost two whole pounds.)

And second, it nearly didn't matter anyway as her mum's refusal to admit that her hip was giving her gip, which would be an acceptance that she is getting old, meant that she claimed that she couldn't walk as far as the bus stop anyway.

'I don't want to walk anywhere where I can't see my destination when I start,' Eva's mum said as she opened the window and started smoking a Silk Cut, half-heartedly puffing the smoke out the window. At this Eva saw red and asked her, perhaps a little too curtly, to smoke outside as they had agreed.

'But it's raining,' her mum had said.

'Then don't smoke' snapped Eva.

Ironically enough that seemed to clear the air for some reason. And the next day, when the rain had stopped, Eva took her mum and Milly down to the stop, which wasn't that far away after all, and they set off to enjoy the Geffrye Museum. At the bus stop a small Turkish-looking man helped lift Milly's buggy on to the bus and then offered his arm to Eva's mum, who took it graciously as he doffed his pork pie hat and helped her on board as well. He then turned and offered Milly a strange Turkish sweet. Milly got all shy and refused it, so Eva stuffed it in the changing bag and apologised. The man simply doffed his hat again and got off the bus and smiled some more.

Mum went home four days later, a day later than she planned, which cost Eva 40 quid, but Eva didn't mind. The Hackney Factor had worked its magic and a trip that could have left a bad smell in the air merely left the faintest whiff of cigarette smoke in her flat.

The 48 arrived and they boarded. Half way towards Hackney Central, Milly fell asleep and Eva sat down. And she smiled to herself a little smile.

***

The Royal Inn on the Park was pretty empty today. Weekday lunchtimes the vibe was chilled and pleasantly not busy. A young couple with a wad of estate agents' details of flats for sale in the area drank Polish beer and chatted on their mobiles. A forty-something creative-looking bloke typed on his Apple Mac and drank Pernod and water with ice. He was eating sausage and mash, which Susan thought must be a drink/food combination too far, but he looked happy. Someone in a waxed jacket read a trashy book with two muddy dogs asleep at his feet. The two people behind the bar were doing the *Guardian* quick crossword at the end of the bar. It felt like a comfy place. A place in which she belonged. She was 33 and a woman and alone in a bar and it felt good. It felt right.

Susan lived just down Victoria Park Road in one of those 70s flats. Flats she had recently discovered were designed by the great Basil Spence, or at least his practice. She'd lived there for ten years and couldn't see her self ever moving anywhere else. 'The Village' – what up-their-own-arse residents of Victoria Park called the collection of shops that huddled around the roundabout at the crossroads of Viccy Park Road and Lauriston Road – had become a little poncey and, well, up-its-own-arse, but it still felt vital and she had made some good friends there. And if The Village itself ever got too much, there was always Broadway Market, an old drovers' track that shepherds used to use to drive sheep to Smithfields back in the day. True, that when Susan had first moved to E9, Broadway Market consisted of one stall selling carrots and cabbage and a dodgy-looking bloke trying to sell crack, but now it had grown into a bustling Saturday market with street food and stalls selling guitars and bikes and olives and hot-smoked stuff and Isle of Wight tomatoes. And, as a consequence, the whole area had perked up and was felt like somewhere that had a soul. Somewhere with an edge still, but somewhere that wasn't a shit-hole. But, on a Thursday lunchtime, the Royal was a lovely place to go and sit in the sun and have lunch and a drink or two.

Susan ordered paté and toast and a large glass of white wine and sat down with her notebook writing a list of things she needed from Tesco's. Normally she'd shop locally or get a delivery, Ocado probably, but she'd taken a few days off work that she was owed in lieu and was going a bit stir crazy in her flat. Her husband tried to take some holiday as well, but he was working on a massive project and he just couldn't get the time off, so she was on her own for a few days, something that she wasn't used to. In fact yesterday the barman in the Pub on the Park, not to be confused with the Royal Inn on the Park, the former being in London Fields the latter by Viccy Park, apologised for not recognising her without her husband in tow: 'You two are a bit of a double act,' he explained, which she thought was lovely and repulsive at the same time.

She thought she'd cook something this afternoon and although her kitchen cupboards and fridge seemed to be full she just couldn't muster up the energy to assemble any of it into anything that might resemble a dish. Instead she thought she'd bake, something she used to do with her mum, and sometimes her nan, on Saturday mornings. Flour, sugar, desiccated coconut and jam were calling and perhaps a few other bits too, and a trip on the 277 seemed a good way to get out for a bit.

She finished her meal and drank the last of her wine and looked out of the great windows down Lauriston Road into Bethnal Green for a bus. The long, straight road dissected the park and at the roundabout by the Crown Gate and The Crown pub a bus was heading her way. Susan grabbed her book and her pen and her bag and left the Royal as quickly as she could without actually running full pelt. The bus stop is about 200 metres from the pub, on the other side of the road and the bus sped past her and screeched to halt leaving her about half way left to go. In her heart Susan knew there would be another bus along in a few minutes and it was a lovely day so she wasn't sure why she was running. Is it something we are taught or is it innate? Nurture or nature? Perhaps there is a bit inside us that harkens back to when we were hunters chasing our prey; can't let this one get away, don't know when the next one might turn up? Kind of the predatory equivalent of the fight or flight thing. Anyway, for whatever reason, Susan darted across the road, which is strangely very wide at that part, and towards the bus. Beep beep beep, she could hear the doors closing and the see nearside indicator cancelling. Arse, she was too late and only just too late too, which is the worst sort of late. Being late by ages is okay, but just missing something is somehow much worse. Just for the hell of it, to finish what she started she supposed, she continued to run up to the bus expecting to see the driver looking over his shoulder for a space to get out and on his way. But instead he was looking at her coming up alongside the bus and pressing the button to open the doors again. A little out of breath, she climbed on, thanked him and pressed her Oyster card against the yellow reader. A satisfying electronic chirrup answered her and she considered herself the luckiest person in Christendom. Not only for the fact that the bus driver waited for her, but because it was sunny and she was off work and she lived in such a great place.

***

In the little wine shop on Old Street, just south of Hoxton Square, Keith was buying a half bottle of Black Muscat. For some reason they only sold the half bottles in the UK and they went down too well. Not that Keith drank particularly a lot, or that he had particularly expensive tastes, he just liked the Black Muscat and had decided a long time ago that money is too vulgar to be only spent on necessities. He'd been in the shop a few times before and liked it a lot. It was well stocked and run by knowledgeable people who enjoyed what they did. There weren't many shops like that about any more: The Algerian Coffee Shop on Old Compton Street; the pipe and cigar shop on Threadneedle Street, Smoker's Paradise or something, not that he smoked any more; and the umbrella shop on New Oxford Street (he couldn't remember the name of that one at all); not many. But this one was his favourite. He eyed the bottles of Cristal Champagne and the cases of Gavi di Gavi and Hennessey XO Cognac and promised himself that he'd drink more – something his doctor wouldn't be pleased about, but an admirable hobby he thought for a fifty-seven-year-old man to take up. He handed the small bottle over the counter to be swaddled in tissue and then gave over his card. The bottle was popped into a bag and the terminal thing handed across for him to pin his chip. 'Pin Accepted' pinged up on the screen and he handed the terminal back. The shop assistant, the man who owned the place thought Keith, had a pained look on his face.

'It's jammed again,' he grimaced and, placing the glasses that dangled around his neck on to his face he picked up a 'waiter's friend' and prised the top off the machine with the little knife. From inside the terminal he slowly pulled a very screwed-up piece of paper and ripped it off with the gusto of a well-trained sommelier refilling an empty glass.

'I'm sorry sir, but I can't see if it's gone through or not. I think it has, but I can't see what it says.' he said offering the pleated piece of paper to Keith which, Keith had to agree, was illegible.

'Do you want me to pay again?' Keith asked.

'I think it's gone through,' the shop owner mused. 'No, sir, perhaps you can have a look at a statement in the next few days and see if it shows up. If not would you mind popping back to pay, if it does then it's all okay.'

Keith thanked the man and left the shop. A 55 bus was coming up the road and Keith boarded it *en route* to the Hackney Empire.

It wasn't until the bus had turned the corner and was half way up Hackney Road, one of the most desolate roads in London thought Keith, that he realised what had just happened. Nowhere else in London but Hackney would a shopkeeper trust him to go back and pay if he hadn't have been charged. 'I'm afraid you'll have to pay again sir and if it shows up twice, please come back for a refund,' is what he would have expected. But Hackney was different. Hackney people were good people: artisans; thinkers; lovers; musicians; writers; artists; and loose cannons. The sort of people who'd trust you to go back and pay if they happened not to have the first time.

His dreamy thoughts were soon put to the back of his mind as the bus driver seemed to be trying to break some world land speed record as he raced past Cambridge Heath Station and up Mare Street. The whole fleet of London buses had been fitted with information displays in the last year or so, with details of what the next stop is going to be. A great invention thought Keith, now no one has any excuse not to get a bus. To make the system even better, a soothing woman's voice accompanies the changing signs announcing the number of the bus, its destination and the name of the next stop. Sometimes, on busy routes, she orders people 'not to stand on the upper deck or stairs' or to 'please move down inside the bus'. Every now and again the bus will be held at a stop and the soothing voice will explain that 'this bus is being held here briefly to help regulate the service'. Perhaps they needed to record a new message thought Keith: 'this bus is being driven at 70 miles an hour to help regulate the service'. Perhaps he'd go online and suggest it.

As the person sitting next to Keith left, Keith shuffled over to allow people to sit down. It really pissed him off when people sat in the aisle seat. Especially when they placed their bag next to them and pretended not to notice anyone wanting to sit down. It was like when you worked in an office – okay, Keith hadn't worked in an office for ages, but he remembered – when you filled your instant coffee cup with water from the crappy electric kettle in the cheaply-furnished 'kitchen area' and then didn't refill it. Have some consideration for other people, was his point. As he slid over he picked up a copy of some free newspaper that had been left behind. What a shit waste of time he thought as he folded it up and moved it on to the seat he'd just vacated. He really couldn't stand the vacuous pseudo-journalism all those free papers were now spouting across London. Okay, their passively right-wing editorial leanings were abhorrent, but what was really wrong with them was their lack of depth. Cute pictures of squirrels that had fallen from trees sat cheek-by-jowl with paedophilia cases and sensationalist *Daily-Mailia*.

And, in this copy, the front page didn't let him down. 'Negative equity a reality for London's home-owners' was the empty headline. He was sure that house prices were not growing as fast as people wanted, but that was surely a function of the fact that people, and especially London people, looked on their house as an investment and not just a place to live.

Keith lived on Cassland Road. Actually he lived in one of the large houses on the semicircular bit of Cassland road just north of Well Street Common. He'd lived there since the early seventies with his partner. (He didn't like the word 'partner', it didn't feel important enough, more suited to how one might refer to an old dog. And as for 'girlfriend'; well that simply too weird for words.) And he considered himself lucky. Not just in the I-live-where-I-want-to-live way, or in the my-house-is-ace-and-still-increasing-in-value way. Keith was lucky because his house had paid for itself – literally.

It was the early seventies and that part of Hackney wasn't particularly upmarket (in fact, no part of Hackney is particularly upmarket even now, not even with the Olympic village spreading its light across east London like a benign dictator of municipal spending) when Keith and Sharon bought their place. In fact, it was a right tip. Previously owned by a Jewish couple who had fled the Holocaust in the years running up to WWII, it seemed like a crazy museum when they had moved in. Dark rooms, old wiring, antimacassars, stale smells and cold comfort. The old couple, after fleeing Herr Hitler's worst and settling in E9 had bought up two sons and a daughter there. The man had died a year before the house went on the market and, as is the case in so many of these close relationships, his wife nine months later. The eldest son sold it to Keith and Sharon for six thousand pounds. The son couldn't bring himself to clear the house, either through laziness or repulsion to the idea of breaking up his family home and Keith and Sharon moved in to a spookily fully furnished house, albeit one furnished in or around 1955.

Keith had never been super house-proud, but the place was like a morgue with the dead couple's stuff everywhere. So, even though they didn't have any furniture of their own Keith and Sharon started to clear the place and make it theirs. Sharon was, after all, pregnant and the cigarette-tainted settee was not what she wanted her son or daughter to play on. First, the drawers and tallboys and cabinets went. They were well made, but not what people wanted in these modern times. Keith got a few quid for them, but that was all. Then the soft furnishings and the curtains and all that stuff. It was hard work actually. The old couple were by no means slovenly, but perhaps their eyesight had deteriorated along with their propensity to clean over the past few years. Dust seemed to pervade and weigh down every atom of every item they moved or threw away or sold or burned. But the armchairs and the sideboards were nothing compared with the rugs. None of the rooms had wall-to-wall, as was the mode those days. Instead threadbare woollen rugs lay heavy in the centre of every space. Rugs that belched clouds of dust if you lifted a corner and dropped them. Keith hated the idea of lifting them, but the idea of his child crawling on them was an even bigger turn off, so he put on a pair of overalls and wrapped a handkerchief over his face and, along with Sharon, began the task of rolling up the rugs.

They started in the front room, on their hands and knees, making a kind of grime-encrusted swiss-roll, all ready to lift up and out, into the back of a Bedford van Keith had borrowed the day before.

'Look, The Beatles take America!' Sharon exclaimed.

In her hand was a browned and crispy copy of the *Daily Mirror* from 1960-something that had been lying under the rug.

In front of them, where the rug had lain was a week's worth of tabloid, carefully spread out like a paper underlay. Keith picked up another page and a large white oblong of paper fell from the sheets. Then another. Sharon lifted the sports page and there were some more.

'These are fivers' Keith acknowledged, incredulously.

'There must be 40 or 50 here' Sharon replied.

She was wrong. There were 328 under that rug and 138 under the equally grimy rug in the back parlour. Then 312 in the hall, 626 stuffed in the unused chimney flue in the bedroom, 52 in a little cubbyhole in the toilet and 234 in an old leather football they found in the attic.

Eight thousand, four hundred and fifty pounds. Okay it was in old money that, since decimalisation, no one could spend, but the banks were still accepting it and exchanging it for bright shiny New Pence.

The house that had cost them £6,000 had made them £2,450. Real money.

Keith felt genuinely bad for anyone stuck in the negative equity trap, especially first time buyers, and he felt a pang of guilt that it wasn't an issue for him.

***

At 1.20 the 48 approached the Hackney Town hall stop from the north and Eva reached down to give Milly a carton of juice and strap her in, ready to get off the bus. At the same time, across the road, directly outside the Town Hall below the one-tonne-a-letter typography that the Hackney Empire wears like a concrete and steel toupee, the 277 and the 55 pull up and Susan and Keith both wait to get off their respective buses. One is blocked by a really much too fat woman with a hundred Argos bags, the other by a frail old man, shaking as he tries to lift himself down the step. As they both manage to get off Eva and Milly have crossed the road and Milly is struggling to get out of her buggy so she can run about in the little square that sits corned by the library, the town hall and the theatre, so her mum reaches down and lets her out. Susan looks at the town hall and remembers her wedding day there. Keith helps the much too fat woman with her bags and sets off towards the Empire.

And that's when it happened.

Although no one person had any idea of the bigger picture and how it all fitted together and the ramifications of what could have happened if any one of them had acted differently.

First, the frail man lost his footing and fell. Eva went over to see if he was okay and, as a consequence, took her eye off Milly, who decided to run across the normally unused road between the town hall and the Empire. Susan turned to walk to the Tesco's on Morning Lane and saw the blue car with a tea-tray spoiler and stickers race around the corner and do a hand-brake turn into the road. At this she yelled. Keith immediately looked up and saw that the car was heading straight for a little girl. He jumped forward and grabbed her and fell forward. Somehow he managed to hold onto her and his wine as the car raced off and two police cars sirened after it.

Then suddenly it was quiet.

And everyone was okay.

And the day, a day peppered with tiny acts of trust and warmth and smiles and helpful people, simply carried on.

HARINGEY
Hollywood

Hollywood

Bobby Nayyar

If there's one thing I love about London, it's that cinemas are still part of communities. They haven't been exiled to the outskirts of the city, they are there with the people, changing like the seasons, struggling just like everyone else.

People raise their eyebrows when I say that my favourite cinema will always be the Hollywood on Wood Green High Road. They then ask if I'm taking the piss. Oh no. You could hop on the Piccadilly line to Leicester Square and pay 21 big ones to watch a film, or get off a couple of stops earlier and watch something arty (read: unintelligible) at the Renoir. On Tuesdays all films at the Hollywood used to cost a Paltrow £4. Sure you'd get the youts talking on their mobile phones, couples thinking it's OK to chatter as long as they don't use English, and frustrated generation y-ers lashing out at said youts. But you also get something rare in Broken Britain: value for money. A reasonable viewing experience tempered by a little noise is a fair compromise. A bit like the NHS.

On Tuesdays, or more precisely, every second Tuesday, I would wake with an uneasy feeling in my stomach, for I – Tarsem Singh – am one of the three million unemployed in this fair green land. Coming on to twelve months, ever since I graduated. Mother is happy her ladhla is back home. Her prodigal. She's been assiduously fattening me up with samosas, tandori chicken, kim mar and sarg. Laundry and ironing. I have a feeling she's trying to Benjamin Button me, it wouldn't be long till I'd be in swaddling, then passing back through the maternal canal. Best place to be. Father hasn't been quite so magnanimous, he's stopped saying it, instead he's formed a new facial expression that says, 'Get a job you beevecouf.' He hasn't even mentioned getting me a job at the factory, that's how disappointed he is. And that's just the start. Every second Tuesday I would go to the Jobcentre Plus on Mayes Road and sign on. No university course prepares you for that feeling.

I'd sugar the pill by popping into the Hollywood after my visit. A matinee screening. Occasionally I'd get lucky and be the only one in the auditorium. Just me, the silver screen and my dreams. Nothing could touch me in those moments. It was during *Star Trek* (the new one with all the youngsters) when all this changed. When Sae Nakamura walked into the Hollywood.

I remember clearly. She entered the auditorium a moment before the lights dimmed, surveyed the room, then walked up the sticky stairs with a quiet dignity and poise. She was tall, wearing a navy blue coat that reminded me of a painter's smock, black hair tied back. For all the choice available, she sat at the end of my row, giving me the faintest of nods as she sat down.

Manny popped into my head. My friend of many years. A believer in NLP and the rules of *The Game*. 'When a woman looks at you, you have a window of opportunity of no more than 3 seconds. After 3 seconds you may as well not exist.' Oh Manny. I waited 127 minutes. Spent most of the film mulling it over. The legitimacy of such a move, the whys and the wherefores of picking a cinema seat, suitable lines of introduction. I got so wound up I missed the end of the film. Sae glanced at me as she gathered her things to go. What a gift. Three more seconds!

'What did you think?' I blurted as I grabbed my jacket and stood up.

'Sorry, I didn't catch you,' she replied. I caught the glint of a smile as I neared her. I repeated my question.

'I thought it was OK,' she said with an American twang, 'It didn't have the kitsch quality of the TV series.'

I nodded, stalling for something else to say.

'Say, would you like to go for a cup of coffee?'

She stifled a laugh and looked at me head to toe, a body scan of sorts.

'That's quite a line,' she said dryly. 'Has it ever worked for you?'

'First time I've used it. I swear.'

'What's your name?'

'Tarsem.'

'I'm Sae,' she said slowly, emphasizing the vowel sounds, sA-Eh.

We made our way to the lobby, emerging to the light of a fine summer's day. Sae looked at me, I looked at her. She was beautiful. Lightly tanned skin, a dusting of freckles, dark eyes, delicate lips. My heart sank. I had that peculiar Asian male trait: thin legs and arms with a rounded belly, a bit like a frog I guess. I wasn't vying with anyone for her attention yet I felt that I had already lost.

'So, do you want to go?' she said, noticing that I had slowed.

Outside the air was peppered with exhaust fumes, kids played hooky, groups of people congealed by bus stops. There wasn't much choice nearby: McDonald's or a Wetherspoons. You gotta love Wood Green.

'Why don't we go here,' I said nodding at the former.

She made an indifferent sound. We bought our drinks and sat upstairs by the windows overlooking the street. Sae told me she had arrived in London a couple of weeks ago. She was studying a summer art course at Central St Martins, was from a town called Matsuyama, which was on the Shikoku section of Japan. Her father was some sort of industrialist. Before London she had been in Paris. Before Paris, New York.

'So what about you?' she asked.

I had been to the Jobcentre. Plus.

'You could say I'm between things,' I muttered.

'What things?' she said with a hint of irony as she lifted the lid of her coffee.

'Today and tomorrow.'

That struck a chord with her, I could see the change in her face, almost as if she was reassessing her opinion of me. Spurred by this I told her that I had always wanted to be a poet, that I wrote and performed compulsively through my student days but had never quite made the transition to something more real.

'This is the challenge of the artist,' she said straightening her back, 'to find a focus. I think I can help you,' she said, taking out a scrap of paper from her bag. She wrote down her email address and mobile number. 'Write me a poem. If I like it, I'll go out with you again.'

With that she was gone.

'And then what?'

'And then she was gone.'

Manny looked down at his steak and shook his head. We were in the Columbian restaurant on Stroud Green Road. The steak was thin but wide, served on a wooden board with rice and a plantain.

'That's the most implausible story I've heard from you yet,' he said taking off his glasses.

I tried to laugh it off.

'It's a classic: boy meets girl, boy and girl drink coffee, girl asks boy to write poem.' I showed him Sae's scrap of paper. I kept it in my wallet where money was supposed to be.

'And have you written your poem?'

'Worked on it for a solid three hours. There's me, then Dante, then Petrarca. I emailed it to her this morning.' Manny lifted his chin. 'No news yet, but I'm hopeful. It's quite a feeling to be writing again.'

He put his glasses back on and cut his steak across the middle with one broad stroke. I was eating salad.

'And what about the email I sent you?'

Fair dues. I had walked straight into that one. I couldn't complain, of all my friends Manny was the only one who stuck by me. We search for unconditional love, but unconditional friendship is a greater gift. He had forwarded me an email about an entry level job going at his … bank.

'I'm thinking about it.'

'Well don't think too long. The deadline's next week. Look, it's just a job. What was it you said when I started?'

I bit my bottom lip. I knew he'd use that line against me.

'I said that even T. S. Eliot worked in a bank.'

Manny took a breath as if to speak. The sound of my mobile beeping interrupted him. I set my smile to smug. It was Sae.

'What did she say?' Manny asked, finally believing me.

'She'd like to see me on Saturday.'

'Where?'

Mother watched me suspiciously as I put on my shoes. I had made a rookie mistake by combing my hair.

'Where are you going?' she asked turning the volume down on the TV.

'Out.'

'Where?'

'Alexandra Palace.'

'Why?'

It went on like this for a couple of minutes. She hadn't bought it, her eyes narrowing, eyebrows raising to divine my intentions. She switched to Punjabi and told me that I better not be doing something naughty. She had me Button-ed to an age of twelve or thirteen.

Sae met me by the pub at Alexandra Palace. She was wearing three-quarter length jeans, ballet flats, and her trademark blue coat. She walked ahead of me, crossed the road, the whole of south-east London enveloping her like a mist. Guided by the torn sound of the wind, we negotiated our way past couples and young children before choosing a dry patch of grass. The sun on its descent behind us, we sat watching the city blinking to a thousand lights ahead.

'In Japan they call people like me a "freeta",' Sae said, sadness in her tone. 'People who are free, but always falling from one thing to another. My father pays for me, wherever I go, whatever I do. When I was nine I came home from juku and found him with another woman. Not my mother. I'll never forget the look on his face. And he'll never forget the look on mine. Two people trapped by a moment, maybe for the rest of our lives.'

She had tears in her eyes. She inhaled and took a piece of paper from her jacket pocket. 'Then there was a line in your poem that reminded me of this:

Like a sycamore seed falling through the years as if in flight.

It's a beautiful line but it reminded of much sorrow.'

'I'm sorry. I didn't mean it in reference to you. I was thinking more of myself. Of how I just can't seem to find a path.'

'Maybe we're not so different then. Maybe that's what an artist is. Someone who thinks he is flying when he is really falling.'

The distance between us closed, Sae leaned her head upon my shoulder and touched my hand. It's hard to think that beautiful people get lonely. We sat in silence, watching the pauses of light spread across London.

'I want to show you my work,' she whispered, grasping my hand.

We walked down the slope, emerged in Muswell Hill where we caught a bus to Crouch End. Something profound had changed in Sae, her face revealed a disquiet mixed with tenderness. She held my hand, and watched me as I watched London unfold from street to street.

Her studio flat was in the top floor of an Edwardian house on the crest of a hill not so far from the Broadway. I waited in the corridor while she made sure everything was tidy. She asked me to come inside. The main room was large, dark wooden floors and small lamps turned on to avoid using the naked bulb hanging from the ceiling. There was a single bed in the corner of the room, and by the only window, which looked out towards Alexandra Palace, was a plan chest that doubled as a sofa. The focus of the room was the wall by the kitchenette, which was covered in drawings. I inspected them like I was in a gallery, while she made some tea.

'I only draw from memory,' she said, her back turned to me. 'It's more interesting when you go back and try to recreate the things you have seen, rather than copy what is in front of you.'

It was uncanny. Each drawing was made in ink, meticulously formed. I was sure I recognised some of the faces from Wood Green. There were the proud Africans and Bangladeshi mothers, the Crouch End couples with baby, pram, and a copy of the *Observer*, the directionless and the driven, all competing for space. It was life.

'Do you like it?' she asked, handing me a mug.

I nodded and told her I recognised some of the people.

'It's what I like about this place. Matsuyama is not like Tokyo or Osaka, you don't get so many different types of people. Here there is always something new around the corner.'

We sat on the plan chest. The sun had long set, the floor lights cast an apologetic light making it feel like we were far more advanced into the night. Sae leaned against me.

'When I saw you at the cinema,' she said a little apprehensively, 'I thought you would be the perfect subject for a portrait. "Man alone in cinema". Something like that.'

'Oh.'

'But then you kept looking at me. You thought I wasn't noticing, but I found it quite cute.'

'Did you draw me?' I asked glancing at the wall of portraits.

She shook her head. 'It's harder for me to draw someone I know. Emotions control memory. Have you ever thought that?'

I placed my mug on the windowsill and held her hand. The room grew darker, the tea turned cold, we both knew we were at that point where I either left or stayed the night. Sae brushed her leg against mine.

'Do you want to?' she asked meekly.

'I don't know. Do you want to?'

'Maybe. It depends if you want to.'

It was the not-lovers-yet fugue, which could have gone on for hours if I hadn't reached out and kissed her cheek, my left hand on the small of her back to bring her body closer to mine.

Ah, the walk of shame. Well, actually it was a walk, bus ride, then walk again down the Haringey ladder. The lights were all on at home. I expected that mother had spent the night fretting and searching for me under beds and in closets. She was standing in the doorway of the kitchen as I opened the front door.

'Where have you been!' she snapped, then reeled off Punjabi expletives. She smacked my shoulder and sniffed near my neck. I had the faintest scent of Sae's perfume on my skin. 'You bescharum,' she continued, 'you go upstairs and take a shower. When you come back down you're getting married,' at which she stormed back to the kitchen to make father his breakfast.

I took off my jacket and shoes and went to the living room. Father was there, for a change he had a wry smile on his face.

'So you finally achieved something?' he said, trying not to laugh, patting the sofa space next to him. I sat beside him and nodded my head.

'If you do things like this, then you can also get a job.'

'I know.'

We both sighed.

'Son, what do you want to do with your life?'

I told him.

'Then go do it,' he said, putting his arm around me.

And that was it. Life went on. I saw Sae only one more time after our night in Crouch End. It wasn't like the movies, we were both awkward and mismatched, no amount of one liners or musical montages was ever going to change that. Mother stopped swaddling me, laundry and ironing stopped first, then my favourite dishes, then came talk of me paying rent. I was one step ahead of them, I got a job as an administrator at an arts charity. A lowly wage and measly work but it left my mind free to fall and to fly. And it kept the people around me happy and secure.

Even the Hollywood closed in late autumn, yet another chapter of my life ending. The cinema came back rebranded, another piece of London's cultural identity lost. One of the screens had been converted to show films in 3-D. I tried it – it didn't seem as real no matter how many CGI swords were thrown at the audience. I took refuge in books and wrote on weekends.

In January of the next year I received a package from Madrid. It was a journal, the kind put together by a collective of artists to give to friends and gallery owners. A postcard of Velázquez's *Las Meninas* marked out a page. The card was from Sae. It read:

Tarsem,
I hope you have been writing. I am still a sycamore seed.
Love,
Sae

The page was a portrait of me sleeping in Sae's single bed. There was a smile on my face. I looked peaceful and happy. The title of the drawing read:

The Poet of Wood Green.

ISLINGTON
Real People

Real People

Ariana Mouyiaris

Barnsbury had changed. And it was questionable if this was for the better. Copenhagen Street was a foreign land where geographical markers (by way of taps and local brew) had been usurped; taken over by profiteers and a new English underclass. The Cloudesley Arms had been converted to flats; King Edwards to The Church on the Corner. The Lord Nelson demolished and the Milford Haven, a Chinese bakery. Not even the Sutton Arms, an old stomping ground for Arsenal supporters, had been saved although salvation could be found (or so its Pentecostal followers preached) within the Gothic walls of the Celestial Church of Christ where baritone and off-key undulations, praising the word of the Lord happened regularly and with gusto in strained falsetto notes that rung off the roof, spilling into otherwise quiet, very Victorian Cloudesley Square.

For the most part, Barnsbury's squares had been opened to 'the people', generous mandates to posterity after the landed could no longer afford their land. Had they known the resultant cultural behaviours that would befall their once prized playgrounds they would, undoubtedly, have questioned their benevolence. Middle-aged mums battled it out with their adolescent daughters, parading their dogs on looping tours of the landscaped grounds. It was a gymkhana of sorts with a tiered point system for pissing on the flower beds: one point for daffodils, three for crocuses and a whopping fiver for roses. Spitting was also game, although this tended to come from the human instead of the canine variety. Despite the fact that the pigeons were still a lovely blue grey: fat and feathered with the white collars of clergymen, their foul-footed cousins – the peskier variety – still hankered around the periphery. And, the same could be said for the neighbourhood's residents.

Charlie had been born in Islington. Born before the speed bumps and the baby prams, the bankers and the bourgeois moved in. His grandmother had bought their terraced house – now worth over a million – for £30 and a scrawled signature on parchment. 'Love' and 'darlin' peppered his speech as much as positive inflections when on the phone and obscenities when transmitting ruthlessly over crackling radio waves.

He had been proclaimed the king of the London minicab: the ringleader. Organising, franchising and operating from his bastion on Cloudesley. The occasional escape to the dusty sands of southern Spain, where his brother-in-law (one of the uncounted but over-numbered English populating its once Cockney-free shores) owns a residence, helps break the damp winters and soggy summers; although not mentally far from home.

North One's brigade of drivers hailed from the far-flung, ex-outposts of Empire: Peter from Jamaica (never to be seen without his soft-knit, green, yellow and red cap despite the cliché of it), Phoenix from Ghana, rechristened to hasten his rise from the ashes – although admittedly Catholic by youthful enticement in the form of colourful, foil-wrapped cavity pleasers – and Sandip, a god-fearing, if not altogether misplaced Bengali, along with the recently uprooted looking for a new life on English soil.

On this particular evening, it is Sandip's lilted English echoing forth from the phone system's tinny sounding speakers.

'Sandi, darlin', I've already told you. 10 Malvern Terrace. Down Thornhill, across from the Albion. North of the park ... yes, the pub ... yes, I know *you* don't give directions based on pub coordinates.'

The thought that Sandip had been in this country ten plus years and still hadn't set foot in one, or ANY, of England's staple establishments, aside from the Buckingham Palace, struck Charlie as odd. It occurred to him that the reverse would be tantamount to never getting a curry in a local curry house on the other side of Kathmandu or Calcutta, or whichever small corner of the world Sandip was from.

In fact, Sandip Achariya Rama Dutta was one of a brood of seven, having landed on this green isle by way of the sixth who had, had the fortune to procure passage from one of the world's most densely populated regions on earth to one of its wettest modern kingdoms.

The exchange over radio waves continues.

'Listen, if I have to give you the directions a third time, you're not going to like where I'm going to tell you to go and, it's definitely not in Islington.'

It was too much for the beginning of his night shift. If there was one thing that Savlon couldn't fix for Charlie, it was miscommunication over the night-waves.

Saturday nights were the worst for this. There would be drunken passengers, potential vomit and occasional violence, not to mention incomplete cab fares. Of course, if the drivers couldn't get their customers to pay, it was hardly his job to cover their losses. Still, he didn't like it to happen as his motley crew had been with him a long time and depended on the difference between a tenner and noner. This, along with the sheer volume of calls, is what brought him back to base every weekend. They needed a figurehead. A man at the helm to steer them clearly through the night. At least, that's what he reasoned when his missus complained about their lost weekend double bill at the local cinema – a megaplex of robust concrete and more acne per square metre than a secondary school classroom – her weekly treat after thirty-odd years married to a warm, if proverbially round, husband.

The truth was, Charlie loved his job. It was his community; and through it, he occasionally got a glimpse of other lives. Like most things for Charlie, it was a case of 'bricks and mortar', the exterior reflecting the interior. This was true for people as much as for buildings, and never more so than with Celeste.

***

Charlie had met Celeste through a peculiar set of circumstances that had at first bewildered, and then endeared her to him. She was a chatty twenty-something fresh out of art school, with an unfortunate 'gullible' gene that was charming, though lamentable. This trusting nature was what had gotten her stranded near the Hackney Downs without cab fare or wallet in the early hours of a cold, January morning, nearly a year ago.

Somehow she had met a group of overly styled hipsters after her shift at a bar in Shoreditch and decided to follow them on to an after party further east. She'd been recently dumped and was flattered by the invitation but wound up with only her phone, a headache and a calling card with the number for North One minicabs in her pocket.

Charlie had arrived to find a forlorn, poorly clothed redhead sitting on a curb without a penny to her name. Although it wasn't his habit, when she told him where she was going (a street away from his own), he felt it would be cruel to leave her there as it was to be his last pickup before heading home. During the ride, she slurred her way through the story and her heartbreak and, by the time he dropped her off, she had promised to pay him back tenfold. The surprising thing for Charlie was that over the next few months she had, in many small and unexpected ways.

There was the large 'THANK YOU' spelled out in apples outside of his house one Monday morning. The handpainted, if slightly wonky, birdhouse installed on the tree in front of his door – a response to his admission of a fondness for *Birds of Great Britain,* an old illustrated tome left to him by his city born but country-souled father. A basket of fresh veg from the Farmers' Market one sunny Sunday and handpicked wildflowers woven into a garland for his daughter on the first of May.

Yes, Celeste was an anomaly for the area.

When foreigners went west of Upper Street, they tended to be Aussi or Kiwi or, occasionally, from south of the river. West of the Gulf Stream was rare, and south of El Paso, rarer, which seemed to suit her just fine.

Celeste was the kind of girl that lit up a room. The kind of girl that wore heavy-set plastic frames to counter her suggestive pout and shuttled along cycle paths (hair blowing wildly) with a grin and a short skirt. She was never to be seen without her signature carmine lips – her one submission to Chanel's range of black capped, overpriced beauty items – or her favourite eBay purchase, a 1987 Raleigh Wayfarer, affectionately named Rust. When not seen along Islington's miles of cycle lanes or in one of Charlie's cabs, she could be found at some of N1's quirkier addresses:

Number 7 Barnsbury Road, site of Hurley Healing – Reiki Healing and Consultation; Complementary Therapy; Mind, Body, Spirit. All Donations welcome.

S. Cohen Costumier and Furrier, Chapel Market – where she could often be seen staring through the shopfront window at countless gaping, taxidermied faces: mongeese, foxes, ferrets and an owl, blue and white china and second hand paperbacks. Amongst the notable classics on the top shelves (Jane Austen's *Emma, Mansfield Park* etc.), and the tat on the lower (*Come Into My Parlour* by an unremembered Wheatley), she tended to take from the middle; and her last trip saw her cycle rack strapped with *When Stars Collide* and *Gemini Contenders.*

Tonight, though, while Charlie is reflecting on their unexpected friendship, she is at the Albion, and she is in love.

***

We zoom into one of the front sash windows of a favourite local. Celeste sits in a repurposed, mahogany church pew, her fiery red curls falling in soft rings around her face. She giggles as she looks up at Bjorn.

'So, are you going to?'

'Going to what?'

'Ask me to have your babies,' Celeste half-joked.

She always did this. A rhetorical question; delivered poe-faced but with laughing eyes.

'Well, isn't the answer obvious?' Bjorn couldn't help but smile.

At this precise moment Jupiter transitions into Pisces and Celeste's phone rings. As she steps out of the Albion to take the call she sees the white leather seat of her bicycle disappear around the corner of Richmond Avenue. Bjorn, whose gaze has followed her out and refocused through the window, sees the departure of three sweatpant-clad youths and the mint-coloured push bike.

Now, Celeste's first reaction is to take off after them, which she does, but, after 100 metres and flimsy ballet flats she collapses, unwilling to see her Rust nicked for scrap metal.

Bjorn finally catches up to her and reaches for a curl on her neck.

'We should call 999.'

But her second reaction is to call Charlie.

***

Back on Cloudesley, the name 'Red' pops up on Charlie's screen, an affectionate nickname for his offbeat neighbour. When Charlie sees Celeste calling he smiles and wonders where he'll be sending her off to this evening. But when he picks up he hears her hysterical on the other end.

'Calm down, darlin'. What's goin' on?'

'They... these kids stole my bike!'

'Where, my love?'

'Just off Richmond ... do you have anyone around who could take me to follow them?'

Before she'd had a chance to utter the last 'em', the radio in Charlie's office crackled.

'Just arrived at Malvern. Awaiting pickup.'

Sandip had finally arrived and, as luck would have it, would be her chariot for tonight.

'Oh, Charlie ... Can I go with Sandip?' He's just around the corner.'

Celeste knew most of the fleet by name as they'd often helped her catch a train, pick up odd bits, for her installations or made sure she made it home after late nights at Marathon Bar, the inevitable end to concerts over in Camden.

'Well, I don't know darlin',' stammered Charlie. 'It's just that ...'

It wasn't so much the logistics of having to rearrange his original pickup but the fact that he knew where she'd probably trail them to. The Bemerton. And he didn't like the idea of that one bit.

Bjorn, having come to a similar conclusion, was definitely not in favour. A Council Estate virgin, he'd never been in one first hand but, from all secondhand accounts, they were not places to enter lightly. The problem was it was impossible to say no to Celeste when she was set on doing something, partially because he hated to see her eyes get all large and glossy when they welled with tears but ultimately because she'd always find a way to do it anyway. And in this case, if she was going, he definitely didn't want her going alone.

We flash back to the phone conversation.

'... Oh, alright. But listen, you be careful and make sure Sandi waits. OK?'

Celeste thanks him as she grabs Bjorn and runs towards Malvern Terrace. There's no way she's giving up Rust without a fight.

'Don't worry about it, darlin'… don't mention it.'

And with that, the chase is set in motion. Bjorn and Celeste arrive at Sandip's silver Saloon, a Peugeot 407 from the late nineties, open the back door and pile in. Celeste quickly brings Sandip up to speed and they head off in the direction the boys have gone, past the terraced houses on Richmond Avenue guarded by Egyptian-inspired sphinxes and obelisks, towards the Caledonian Road.

***

The Bemerton Estate sits squat in the middle of an area once described as 'little Belfast', the unsightly border to leafy Barnsbury. It is a no man's land on the west side the Caledonian Road: a gutter that carves the course from King's Cross to Holloway, characterised by the bookies and copycenters that fill most rundown high streets. Terrorised by a gang called the 'Untouchables' in the late nineties, the Hollywood dramatisation had passed but not the legacy of its 'anti-social' youths. Compared to its parochial cousin, The Barnsbury Estate, Bemerton's brutalist, sixties sensibility lent to its reputation as harder stuff.

As they pull up to the junction, Celeste spots one of the boys from the gang.

'Sandi, you can drop us off here, you can't take the car any closer and we're going to lose them.'

Although he knows she's right, he's hesitant.

After a pause.

'OK. I'll wait for you here. But be careful.'

She nods and looks to Bjorn.

The camera pans as we see them get out and run after the boy, crossing the pedestrianised entrance to the estate. Now, if they'd had a chance to look at the landscape around, and judged it by Charlie's 'bricks and mortar' meter, they would surely have thought twice but, they were young and, at least one of them was reckless so, instead of stopping on Tulloch Street and turning around, they go in. Past the primary coloured map of the estate and the signs reading 'NO BALL GAMES', *completely ignoring the metres of coiled barbed wire covering the building opposite: a fortress by geographical default.*

Celeste can't imagine why anyone would want Rust. As the name implies, he had been a purchase of love not practicality and his value lay in nostalgia and aesthetics, not in hardware. If they stole him it was just for the sake of stealing. Perhaps idealistically (perhaps due to the cider on tap), she felt she had a solid chance to reason with the culprits.

We follow them as they pass under a covered walkway with a recognisable green and white sign - the telltale mark of Islington Council – that reads, Coatbridge House. Its low overhang makes the transgression onto private property more unwelcoming.

'I wonder if that's for their safety or for ours,' Bjorn mutters.

He glances at Celeste's face and instantly feels sorry for the comment. He gives her a small, reassuring smile and hopes they won't find anyone on the other side.

They reach an opening and in the darkness, her skin seems luminous; ethereal against the dark courtyard. The fluorescent lit terraces and stairwells give the place an ominous feeling, casting a sickly yellow light that, although installed for safety, suggests otherwise. Perth House looms in the distance, a mix of pebbledash, concrete and glass. As they approach, a young boy of about 10 steps out of the shadow and shakes his head.

'Listen, are you looking for something around here?'

'A bike,' Celeste replies. 'My bicycle was stolen from up the road and I would like to ask for it back. Or to buy it back ... I just need to speak with whoever took it. Can you help?'

The boy looks at her skeptically; he's never seen any of the older boys return anything. But as a young boy, he feels the inexplicable attachment to metal modes of transport that don't need a license.

'Alright, I'll see what I can do. But not promisin' anything, alright? ...Y'understand?'

She nods in reply. And they wait while he disappears.

Five minutes go by and they are getting ready to give up. The courtyard is deserted except for a few lone tenants trickling into the compound. Just as Bjorn is about to suggest they make their way back to Sandip the boy reappears.

'Well, first time they might make a deal. But they say it's gonna cost you fifty quid. Not a penny less.'

Celeste's eyes flash with a mix of anger and then soften.

'Oh ... ugh. alright then. Here.'

Celeste reaches for her wallet and then remembers she left it in the pub with her bag.

'Shit. Bjorn, think you could spot me?'
'Of course, let me see what I have.'

He reaches into his back pocket and pulls out some notes.

'Here. And hurry back.'

He extends his hand to the boy who grabs the money and is off like a shot. Celeste sighs, walks up to Bjorn and rests her head on his chest.

'Thanks for coming with me,' she breathes into his shirt. 'At least that was all they wanted.'
'Do you really think I'd leave you to come alone?'

Bjorn reaches to stroke her hair.

'I know, but still. It means a lot to me. I know that thing is a piece of crap but I just … well, you know how much I love Rust.'
'I know.'

The temperature has dropped and they both are beginning to get cold. There isn't a sign of the boy anywhere and it's been nearly 10 minutes. They decide to look where he ran off but all the walkways are deserted and the corridors quiet except for the whine of electricity and distant sound of a scooter engine wailing down a neighbouring street.

'Listen, I think we should get out of here.'
Celeste looks up at Bjorn's tall worried eyes, takes his hand and they walk back the way they came – in and out of the underpass and to the spot where Sandip had left them.

***

After the incident, Celeste contemplated leaving Barnsbury. Although she loved it, on numerous occasions she saw ASBO toting teens clipping locks and trying to hot-wire scooters. Once she had even called 999 (the only time in her life) and they had questioned her for longer than the amount of time it would have taken them to send someone over. She felt degraded and realised that it was rare that she saw any child over the age of 10 who didn't look like he was getting up to mischief of some sort: trying to talk loudly over their counterparts, boast or intimidate. She even had a pack of boys throw snowballs at her as she walked home one night.

Charlie said they had no respect. None for anyone but themselves.

But it was more than that. They just weren't being taught it somehow and, that made her sad; more so than the loss of her Rust.

It wasn't till April that she was walking home and spotted him. His mint, slightly heavy-set frame (with its signature purple stripe and white leather seat) was parked outside the West Library, near the corner of Thornhill Square.

When she approached him, she realised he had been fixed with a new lock and, as all seasons change, that he had found a new home. Although she'd only toyed with the idea of moving, somehow she knew it was a sign and that it was time for her to look for a new home, too. She placed her hand on the cold metal handlebar and closed her eyes briefly. Then, without turning back, she walked briskly past the square with purpose, a smile curling the corners of her crimson lips, ready to find her new corner of London.

CITY OF LONDON

While the City Sleeps

While the City Sleeps

Angela Clerkin

The metal is cold to the touch. I haven't worn gloves. So many times I've driven across London Bridge and never noticed that the granite walls have a metal shelf on the top. I hoist myself up, cold palm on colder metal, these black drill trousers don't have much stretch in them and I think it's typical that I look so ungainly at this moment. My frozen fingers are gripping tightly to the edge as I peer over and look down. My stomach flips even though it's not that big a drop into the dark, murky water. Apparently it's the undercurrent that will suck me under. I take a deep breath.

I died the day that he did, it's just that my body kept going and his didn't. He was only 49. The biting easterly wind is stinging my face and my eyes water. He would have said you're about to commit suicide but still you have time to stop and complain about the weather. I'm a hothouse flower, I would have replied. And I don't belong here in this cold city without you.

I regret having left it until this last possible night. I wonder if cowardice is the right word to describe my inaction. The act of killing oneself requires energy and drive. I used up almost every drop of fuel caring for him and now my tank is empty. I would rather just cease to exist. I want to lie down and never wake up. Why didn't I choose tablets?

Tomorrow I would have been 50. This way both of us will always be 49.

Ethna Carroll's lover, Sean, died three years ago and she has never recovered. She didn't believe she would ever recover. Recover a sense of purpose or belonging. The bus driver's friends fell away while she was being his nurse; his illness was ugly and he hadn't wanted to share it with anyone else. And afterwards, when Sean was gone, she had nothing left to say. And no-one knew how to reach the unreachable woman.

I remind myself that I didn't plump for the tablets because I throw up easily and might inadvertently save my own life. So leaping into the treacherous Thames it is. I stand up and notice how so many new glass-fronted offices have inched their way in between the grand old off-white stone buildings. Bright lights even at 3am St Paul's to my right and Southwark Cathedral to my left – just the heathen Ethna Carroll in the middle, on the bridge. Piggy in the middle. Piggy about to become bacon. Your jokes are so bad, you deserve to die, I can hear Sean teasing. Only in reality I can't hear him say anything. Nobody has spoken a word to me in a very long time.

And then they did. Someone called out to her.

Ethna had started her shift earlier that night at London Bridge station and driven through the deserted City streets all the way to Friern Barnet. Long gone were the daytime suits worn by lawyers and financiers travelling to and from Bank station. The night bus is all about continuing the party from the pubs and clubs – noisy, bustling teenagers laughing and flirting with each other. The bus driver envied the confidence and bravado of youth, their sense of ownership of the City at night. And it added to her sense of isolation that none of them ever seemed to notice her. The woman who cleaned up their vomit and made sure they got home warm and safe.

At 3.28am she set off from London Bridge station for her next journey – only this time she stopped half way across the river. She parked in the bus lane and put on her hazard lights to signal the N43 had broken down. With all her strength gathered, Ethna stood on the bridge wall and took a step nearer to the edge, a step nearer to the end. And then she heard a voice calling out to her, 'Turn again, Ethna Carroll.' She turned and saw an old man dressed in a cape trimmed with ermine, and holding a cat.

'I nearly gave up too. I believed I had lost everything, but when I heard my name called I turned around as I was bid. And I'm glad, otherwise I'd have missed my chance to become Lord Mayor of London three times.' The elderly man smiles at her, his eyes twinkling. Ah! Dick Whittington, she realises. He must be in a pantomime nearby. Ethna is staring but saying nothing so his next gambit is an invitation to come for a walk with him in exchange for the keys to the City. 'Just a few hours. What have you got to lose?' My nerve, my resolve, she thinks but doesn't say. He jangles the keys. 'You were envious of the kids on your bus and their sense of belonging.' He walks towards her holding his hand out and she finds herself taking it and climbing down off the wall.

He was telling her he was *the* Dick Whittington, born 1352 or thereabouts, as they walked across the bridge and turned right into Eastcheap and right again into Pudding Lane. When he paused to look down at the cobbles, Ethna said: 'They're not paved with gold, you know,' and he grinned at her indulgently.

'This spot was exactly where Thomas Farynor's bakery stood in 1666. It caught alight in the darkness of night and started the Great Fire of London.' He tells her in technicolour detail about the flames ravaging the City non-stop for three days, consuming 13,200 houses and 89 churches, 'including St Michael Paternoster Royal where I was buried. Not that they could find my body when they went searching for it in 1949. They only found a mummified cat where my body should have been.' Ethna turns to look in the direction of the church, but instead sees the Monument right in front of her. 'Built by Sir Christopher Wren and dedicated to the Great Fire. It has 133 steps. Do you want to go up?' he asks her. That settles it, she thinks, he is definitely one of those tourist guides that likes to dress up, get into character and boast enthusiastically about how much he knows.

He doesn't wait for an answer; instead the elderly gentleman disappears up the spiral stone staircase. 'Do you have a favourite fruit, Miss Carroll?' He calls over his shoulder. . 'I'm partial to pineapples,' he continues as he climbs. She is reluctantly following him. 'The first one I ever had was in 1832 in the City of London Club on Old Broad Street with Sir Robert Peel.'

'This is all a bit out of your era, isn't it?'

'Ever since I died in 1423 I've make an effort to return to my manor once a year, catch up on the City news.'

202 feet up in the air, and trying to catch her breath, Ethna found her companion sitting on the ground and chatting with his friend Charles, an old black guy wrapped up in a blanket. '… Marty lashed out at his new girlfriend a few weeks back,' explained the homeless man, 'no sign of him since.'

'Ale and anger, it's a terrible combination, Charles. Do you know what happened to the girl?'

'Broken arm. Patched up and back out sleeping on the steps of St Stephen's most nights.'

'It's a hard city. Hard and ugly.' said the bus driver.

Charles looked up at Ethna, a suspicious stare was exchanged, but their common companion introduced them and the frost melted very slightly. 'Look around you, Miss, at the grandeur and the decrepit, the new and the old living side by side. The stoic, the falling down and the newly born.' Ethna leaned over the railings and wondered if he was talking about buildings or people. 'And listen out for the stories carried on the wind by the ghosts that were here before us. Some of it's ugly I grant you, but some of it takes your breath away.'

'Have you ever seen the beautiful stained glass window over at St Michael's?' interjected Dick. He winked at Charles who laughed and then coughed, a deep hacking cough.

'The Mayor and his cat immortalised! Just to the right of the front door.' Charles managed to gasp. 'He thinks this City is all about him!'

Dick asked his ailing friend if he had thought any more about going to a shelter, at least until it got warmer. The old man shook his head. 'Ever since you gave me the keys to the City, Sir, I have made this perch my night-home. I'm in my element with the elements.'

Charles recounts how he was admiring his metropolis from this vantage point back in the early nineties when he was literally blown off his feet. An IRA bomb blew up the Baltic Exchange where the Gherkin now stands. St Mary Axe, clarifies Dick. Locally known as the crystal phallus, adds Ethna. 'A tremendous, thundering explosion, and the Monument was actually shaking beneath my feet. I was almost deafened by the sounds of glass smashing, and brick and cement crashing all around. I thought the world was ending.'

Dick picks up the 'disaster story' baton and tells tales of the Black Death, which killed about 30,000 people in London (and two million in England), around the time he was born in Gloucestershire. When young Richard arrived in London in 1379, seeking his fortune, the streets still smelt of death, disease and bad sanitation. He tells his sceptical audience that even then he had suspected rats carried the disease and that is why he brought his cat Tommy with him everywhere.

Ethna is half listening to their stories as she continues to watch the snail-like progress of the cleaning truck on the road below, now slithering towards the Bank of England on Threadneedle Street. She'd never noticed before that the majestic building doesn't have any windows on the ground floor. And next to it are the steps down to the tube station.

The bus driver remembers her mother talking about the Biltz, and how she and her family had escaped death because her brother had twisted his ankle. They hid under the bed at home one January night in 1941, instead of going to the shelter as usual at Bank station. There was a direct hit and

56 people died in the underground that night.

Stories carried on the wind by the ghosts that were here before us.

Ethna felt suddenly cold, she shivered and put her hands in her pockets. Her turned-off mobile phone was sitting guiltily inside the right one. She thought of Gareth, the driver on the next night bus, worried that he might have reported her abandoned vehicle.

My City guide was halfway down the staircase before he'd called out to me. I smiled goodbye to Charles, and found the going down much easier on my thighs than the going up. We walked alongside some of the remains of the old City wall and happened upon a drunk student pissing against it. Dick told me he had built London's first public lavatory called 'Whittington's Longhouse', which relied on the Thames cleansing it at high tide.

'Those stories you and Charles were telling – fire, bombs, plagues and disasters – you hardly make a case for me sticking around.'

'It's all part of the tapestry, Ethna.'

As he led me through London's dark alleyways and small winding roads, I was wearing the eyes and ears of a tourist and not walking in the City where I was born, walking on roads my Irish father helped build. Lights twinkled and gargoyles grimaced, I was discovering a night-time wonderland.

We sauntered through Leadenhall Market, a dark red wrought iron structure that the old man informed me he had purchased for the City back in 1411. It looked more Victorian to me but I wasn't going to argue. Charles was right; he really does think the City is all about him. I told Mr Whittington that it was now famous for being Diagon Alley in the first Harry Potter film. That made him sneer and I smiled. We saw a couple kissing as they leant up against the butcher's window. I recognised the woman by her red hair and uniform. 'She's a nurse at Guy's hospital, just over the bridge,' I whisper to my companion. 'She often gets on the final bus of my shift. I think she lives near Highgate Hill.'

'There's a monument to me and Tommy on that hill. It's where I heard the Bow bells calling to me to turn around. Perhaps they'll put a monument on London Bridge for you?' This time I sneered and he smiled. He took my hand and held onto it as we left the market, proceeded down Whittington Avenue (of course he drew my attention to the road sign), and onto the deserted Lime Street. I was slightly embarrassed by his gesture but at the same time I liked it. I felt looked after; his hand was coarse, but warm and sure.

The erstwhile Mayor stopped briefly to talk to a couple of security guards at the 'Inside Out' building. The bus driver slipped her hand away from her escort and started to walk around Lloyd's futuristic structure. She knew how it felt to have all her innards on show. Funny how it looks spectacular on a building but unattractive on a 49-year-old woman, she thought. She should be over it by now but the tears just keep flowing. And her bursts of anger are not attractive. Sean no longer around to tell her, 'You are beautiful, warts and all.' Sean no longer around to laugh when she replied with a witch's cackle: 'Warts and all!!'

'Now it's time for victuals,' her City guide announced as they crossed the road and walked towards Bishopsgate. Ethna launched into a rant about hating insurance companies, the financial traders, and the fat cats who make money from other people. 'And the security guards you were just talking to are mugs, earning a pittance while their bosses are tucked up warmly in their mansions.'

'Or perhaps they are providing for themselves. Perhaps they like their jobs. Or maybe one of them hates it but is planning to resign as soon as he gets his own fashion business up and running. You'd find out more if you actually talked to them.'

'No point.'

'And for your information *I* was a fat cat, Ms High and Mighty. I made a lot of money trading silks and velvet from Africa and the Far East.'

'I hate you too.'

They strolled in silence for a while before he asked her if she had been thinking about Sean. Was that why she was so angry? No reply. They continued walking without words. Still holding hands.

My temper started to cool and I wanted to lighten the mood so I joked about making sure my last meal on earth was a good one. I told him I needed to build up my strength to climb a wall and jump in the river. (That was my best attempt at levity.) My companion said the finest possible eatery was moments away, and just as I started expressing my doubts about the existence of this restaurant he opened the door to Polo's 24-hour café.

Rosa, the Italian waitress, threw her arms around the old man, welcoming him back. As they caught up on family news, Ethna looked round the long and narrow café and sniffed the delicious aroma of homemade cooking. The patrons were a lively, chatty mixture of uniformed police officers, late-night party revellers, and foreign visitors still on a different time zone.

As their food arrived Dick sat down opposite her, 'Look around, these are your people Ethna; night people, the ones that keep the City going while everyone else sleeps. You're part of the tapestry – an important part – maybe you just need to pull on the thread a little tighter and bring the people closer to you.' Ethna didn't reply, she was too busy eating seafood spaghetti, now aware of how hungry she had been.

And then Carlo the chef appeared, all smiles, carrying a pineapple upside-down cake with one lit candle placed in the middle. 'To celebrate the yearly visit of our most valued customer, Mr Whittington, the true Mayor of London.' Dick blew out the candle, as Carlo sat down with them at the table and served three portions with cream. Ethna listened and watched as the chef questioned the man with the ermine-trimmed cape and heavy gold chain all about medieval London. He showed no signs of doubt that their companion was the real Dick Whittington. She wondered if everyone was in on this elaborate hoax. And then she took a mouthful of the pineapple upside down pudding and suddenly she no longer cared.

On their way out Dick collected a food bag and kissed Rosa goodbye for another year. This time Ethna linked her arm through Dick's as they walked in companionable silence. She had missed the warmth of another human being. A couple of girls in miniscule skirts and towering heels shouted from across the road that they hoped the old fella had won the fancy dress prize. Ethna laughed heartily.

They walked past the Mansion House and as they turned the corner they could see a small shape lying on the steps of a church. Dick gave Ethna the food parcel as he thought the girl might not welcome a strange man approaching her. 'And be gentle,' he warned her, 'she is a wounded soul.'

As she got closer to St Stephen Walbrook, Ethna saw that the sleeping drifter had her left arm in a sling. She wondered if it was the woman that Charles had been speaking about. Ethna moved the crumpled tin foil, lighter and spoon away into the corner. She checked the girl's breathing and was relieved she was OK. She laid the food parcel on the next step down and softly covered the young woman with the discarded blanket and stroked the hair from her face. The middle-aged woman sat quietly with the homeless waif and then without waking, the girl's fingers reached out for the corner of Ethna's jacket and held on tight.

Ethna looked up and next to the church door was a plaque commemorating the origin of the Samaritans in 1953. They held their first meetings downstairs in the crypt and their aim was *'to befriend the suicidal and despairing.'* The bus driver began to wonder if her City guide led her here deliberately and her eyes searched for the guilty party. But there was no sign of him. How long has she been sitting here? Where is he?

Suddenly worried, Ethna gently extricated herself from the young woman's grip and went in search of the old man. She ran down empty roads and deserted cobbled streets to no avail – she was furious – and madder still that the pantomime line 'ten minutes and still no sign of Dick' popped into her head. Now was not the time for bad innuendo. She stopped suddenly in the realisation that he had abandoned her.

In full fury Ethna marches back to the bridge. The sun is about to rise. No way, she thinks. She will not be thwarted. She stuffs her hands in her pockets, mobile phone in the right one – and a set of keys in the other. She takes them out and examines the strange dirty silver bunch hanging from an antiquated chain. 'Stupid old man had his fun and then buggered off,' she mutters. And then she sees the N43 is in front of her, the lights still blinking. Sadness descends, replacing anger.

Cold hands on colder metal – looking down into the murky water. She remembers it's the undercurrents that will kill her. And then, just as she is about to jump, she looks over at St Paul's. Ethna cannot believe her eyes: there are two gold pineapples on top of the smaller domes of the west wing. Pineapples. Dick must have known she would see them. She cannot take her eyes off the gilded fruit.

Fifteen minutes later Ethna is back in the driving seat. She honks her horn loudly as she passes the Monument on her right and hopes that Charles can hear her. As she crosses Threadneedle Street she remembers Dick Whittington's words:

'You are part of the tapestry, Ethna.'

She puts her foot down and resolves to pull on the thread a bit tighter. Perhaps later today she will buy a cake to share with her co-workers – to celebrate her 50th birthday.

SOUTHWARK

Parting Gift

Parting Gift

Charlotte Judet

High in a plane tree a London pigeon balances precariously on its one good foot. Silently it expels a ball of excrement and flies off. Southwark Cathedral and the steely winter sky lend the scene a moment of grace; then the pigeon lands in the gutter and takes its fill from last night's abandoned kebab.

Blinking as she moves from the daylight into the covered Borough Market, the tall Swede is oblivious to the bird dropping drying to a crust on her hat. Lucky for some. Intent on buying something, anything, she barges her way between the tourists, students and zealous anti-supermarket shoppers, around whom mothers slalom buggies and wish that they'd left before it got so busy. Her new boyfriend, a pack horse for souvenirs from Tate Modern, the Clink Museum and the Globe, follows a few steps behind.

The visitors from Scandinavia pick their way around fallen falafels, organic ketchup and well-chewed gum. They tread on 150-year-old cobbles, beneath which lie layers of earth and traces of Roman remains; soil and clay that has not been disturbed for centuries. This cool, dense mass surrounds the network of pipes placed there courtesy of Bazalgette's endeavour and the sweat of Irish navvies. The London sewers: one of the seven wonders of the industrial world. And as they emerge from the Market, blinking once again, within the dark of one of these dank and putrid pipes the eighty-first millionth rat in Britain is born, squirming, blind and fondant pink.

Ratus norvegicus. The Norway rat, brown rat, common rat, sewer rat, Hanover rat. Although nothing to do with Norway as it happens. Or Hanover. The Brits were having a spat with the Germans in the 18th century, which is the story behind that one; nobody's quite sure why the Norwegians have the dubious pleasure of official recognition in the nomenclature. Brown, common and sewer though – say no more.

>><<

You're never further than eight metres from a rat in London, so people say. This is unlikely to apply if you are on the 14th floor of a tower block though (even when it is the Elephant and Castle), which is where Selwyn Mathers is being given some bad news by Ron Hammond, Head of Environmental Services, Southwark Division.

'I'm sorry, Selwyn. I really am. I know you don't want to retire yet but the situation at the moment means, well, costs just have to be cut … It's come from the very top I'm afraid.'

Ron knits his fingers together, then separates them, folds his arms and digs his nails into his palms. He looks pleadingly at Selwyn who sits passively in his chair, his slim, white hands resting on his thighs. He can tell that Selwyn isn't going to make this easy for him.

'Would you like me to explain the redundancy package now, or would you rather read this first and come back to me with questions? You only need to work next week out then you're free to enjoy yourself and you never need to see another rat again!'

Selwyn's eyes narrow at his boss's nervous laughter. Ron waves the envelope containing the letter signed by none other than the Secretary of State for Environment, Food and Rural Affairs in Selwyn's direction, hoping to distract Selwyn from his face, which he can feel has turned a revealing shade of scarlet.

'39 per cent,' states Selwyn.

'Sorry? What was that? 39 per cent ... ?' Ron's eyebrows are raised but his spirits are anything but.

'That's the increase in rats in the last five years. Those that count these sort of things say there are probably 15 million in London alone. I reckon there's more. A lot more.'

This is the most Ron has ever heard Selwyn say. He has a sneaking suspicion that it might also be the most Selwyn has heard himself say for some time too, as the rat catcher looks as surprised by his outburst as Ron is. Ron seizes the opportunity and speaks in his most authoritative manner while a miasma of bewilderment still hangs over Selwyn.

'Once again, I am deeply sorry, Selwyn, I really am. It's been a pleasure working with you.'

Ron walks to the door, opens it, and thrusts the redundancy envelope towards Selwyn, who takes it without saying a word.

>><<

There is an unseasonable warmth to the day and the sunlight illuminates the discrepancy between the developers' hoardings, which show pictures of the regeneration project – all pavement cafés and street art, cyclists and user-friendly architecture – and the cracked concrete that is endemic to the area. Stepping deftly between a broken bottle and a pile of dog shit, Selwyn walks purposefully, hands deep in his pockets, head down. The Piccadilly of south London. That's what the Elephant and Castle used to be known as, before the German bombers did their worst and the council finished the job off with their slab-block estates and electricity substation. The shopping centre, built in the early 60s, was the first of its kind in Europe. Now its red elephant stands forlornly at the entrance to the building that is regularly voted the ugliest in the country, while on the street weary immigrants buy bruised fruit from a stall as bendy buses disgorge the students and the old onto the litter-strewn pavements.

The bell attached to the post office door rings with a cheerfulness that belies the crumbling interior and the notice that heralds its demise. Selwyn supposes it won't make any difference to him that this post office is closing down; he won't be passing this way after next week anyway. He buys one 56 pence stamp and an airmail sticker for a postcard to his daughter, Alice. That he has a daughter at all is still a source of wonder to him. His liaison with her mother had been, like all of his relationships, brief, and it was a shock to both of them to find that such a fleeting few weeks of something that neither of them would have described as passion had resulted in the creation of another being. Although he had enjoyed being around Alice, Selwyn was no good at the hands-on stuff. He tried to abandon himself wholly to the likes of horsey-horsey but Alice's squeals of delight alarmed rather than delighted him, and he felt awkward bathing and changing the squirming child. When Alice's mother told him that she and the one-year-old Alice were going to emigrate to Australia he was in part relieved. Years later, as he watched a documentary about an autistic man's difficulty in raising his child, hot, fat tears ran down his cheeks and he sobbed like a baby.

Unsurprisingly father and daughter have never been close – 10 thousand miles has seen to that – but they have built their own peculiar relationship based on postcards sent religiously on the third Friday of each month. For a time Alice suggested that Selwyn move to Australia. In her postcards she had painted a picture of a country filled to bursting with pests of all shapes and sizes, just waiting for Selwyn's many and various extermination methods. In return Selwyn pointed out the dangers of Australian pests (100 types of venomous snake for example). He was going to stick with the brown rat, thanks all the same.

Not that rats aren't dangerous. Hantavirus pulmonary syndrome, rat bite fever, Weil's disease and viral hemorrhagic fever are just some of the exotic-sounding diseases that can occur following a close encounter with a rat. Selwyn knows them all, in detail. And of course there's the rat's most notorious claim to fame – the Black Death. Strictly speaking the black rat was more to blame for that medieval show-stopper, but the fleas that caught a ride on the rats' backs weren't choosy. Black or brown made no difference to them.

>><<

Selwyn walks the mile or so to the river via the back streets. He finds an empty bench with a view of Tower Bridge and scans the footpath for police before removing an apple and a knife from his coat pocket. He's been carrying the knife with him since he was 10 years old. It is the last gift his father gave him. He's never had any trouble from it but he knows that these days he has to be on his guard from young coppers itching to give out a caution. He peels the apple skin in a perfect spiral, then cuts the apple into segments and swiftly cores them, despite the bluntness of his blade. The apple skin falls to the floor and immediately a mangy pigeon limps over and pecks at it, hopefully. Selwyn leans back and eats the apple, following it with one finger of a Kit Kat. Closing his eyes, he lets the last of the sun's rays warm his eyelids. Rats are on his mind. He can almost hear them in the interlinking tunnels that he knows are a few feet below him; a motorway for rats that links the river to the executive homes, the parks to the council flats, the museums to the million pound houses. Rich or poor, rats don't care. Scuttling rats, their claws a blur, rubbing their oily fur against the brickwork, leaving a scented map to guide them home. Baby rats, suckling on their mothers for few weeks; a month or so later and they are ready to breed themselves. Old rats, wise to the ways of the rat-catcher, fighting for the right to mate – a screeching ball of fur and tail …

'Excuse me?' Selwyn opens one eye, then another, his reverie broken. A young, blonde couple stand before him. 'Please could you take a picture with us and the bridge in it?'

Selwyn nods. The couple stand shoulder to shoulder and the girl takes her hat off and fluffs up her hair. She nudges the boy with her elbow and he obligingly puts an arm around her. Selwyn raises the camera and moves it until they are framed between the two towers. He presses the button, not once but twice, then hands the camera back.

The couple walk off, the boy a few paces behind, laden with bags, and Selwyn too leaves the river for the roads. The evening air is chilly and he buttons his coat to the neck and quickens his pace, keeping an eye out for the 185 bus that will take him home to Camberwell, home to his tea and his nature documentaries, where he'll swap boots for slippers, sharpen his knife and make himself something tasty to eat.

>><<

The pigeon turns its head to watch as Selwyn fades into the gloaming, then gives up on the apple peel and hops onto the river wall where it appears to contemplate a short, sharp exit from its miserable existence with the help of the swirling eddies and the rising waters. Having had a change of heart, or so it seems, it takes off again, wings clapping, and ascends over City Hall then heads south. Somewhere in its DNA are the residues of racing pigeon, and it flies on as the light fades, following the Old Kent Road then turning west, with Peckham beneath it. The scent of fried onions and burgers rises into the air but the pigeon does not stop. Over the tower blocks and the traffic-choked streets it goes, oblivious to the changes in scenery below, for already it has left gritty London behind and is passing over East Dulwich, heading for the leafy and salubrious Dulwich Village, with its boutique shops and picket fences, heritage signposts and mothers who lunch. Finally, its one good foot outstretched, it comes to a stuttering halt on the roof of the new loft extension of what one of the area's many estate agents would describe as 'a stunning and substantial detached property,' within which tempers are fraying.

'For Christ's sake Donald, just choose one. I'm not asking you to multitask but it would be helpful if you could do just one thing at a time.'

Donald plucks a tablecloth from the 19th century chest and spreads it on the table before glaring at his wife and slamming the door as he leaves the room.

Caroline stirs the casserole with a vengeance. She'd sent Rosa to the butcher's for one kilo of venison but the stupid cow had, for some inexplicable reason – considering she was born and bred metric – returned with one pound of the stuff so Caroline was having to make up the difference with all the mushrooms that the corner shop could provide. She sprinkles another tablespoon of flour over the sorry mixture, hoping to thicken it up and hide the paltry ingredients, before swearing in the direction of the kitchen clock and running upstairs to get changed.

'Darling, help me with this zip would you? Are you sulking? Oh please don't, you know how stressed I've been at work. I'm sorry, I really am. After tonight, if it all goes well, we can plan a holiday, a bit of winter sun. I've got that Green Earth conference in Madagascar in February – I'm sure I can blag you a seat on the flight. And after the reshuffle... honestly, darling, I really, really do think that Gerald has me in mind for Foreign Secretary! I can sniff it, god, it's so fucking close, I know it. And did I tell you, they're going to let the next FS use Chevening after all! There's some plan to make it look less like a grace-and-favour pad and more like a hotel so that the baying masses don't go all moat and duck house on us, but to all intents and purposes we'll have a 115-room mansion in Kent to party in at the weekends – imagine! Let's just make sure we butter the Clarksons up tonight. Jonathan's word is worth its weight with Gerald. I'll be flirting outrageously with him so feel free to do the same with that ghastly wife of his.'

This cheery invitation is spoken as Catherine pulls on her Louboutins with one hand and applies lipstick with the other. Seconds later she is already downstairs, an apron protecting her low-cut dress, a wooden spoon in her hand. A 21st century knight preparing for a dinner-party battle. Donald lies back on the bed and closes his eyes. He has half a minute of blissful silence before Catherine's screams leave his daydream in tatters.

'Oh my god! Donald! DONALD! There's a rat, a bloody rat in the kitchen!

Donald mutters 'what am I going to do?' in a bad West Indian accent and puts his head under the pillow. By the time he makes it downstairs Catherine is standing on a chair shouting into the phone.

'I know what bloody day it is and what bloody time it is but I need someone to come out now, this minute. Not tomorrow, not next bloody week. Come on Ron, after all the tight spots I've got you out of this is the least you can do in return. Pay them triple for all I care, just sort something out right now.'

'What on earth is the point of being in charge of these people if you can't pull a favour once in while,' spits Catherine as she hands the phone to Donald. 'Now help me down from here. These shoes aren't designed for heights.'

>><<

Selwyn stares at the ringing phone for a while. His old-fashioned Bakelite telephone's fresh-from-the-box shine is through lack of use rather than regular cleaning. He mutes David Attenborough's excited whisper then picks up the receiver and listens as Ron makes him an offer he can't refuse. Then he switches off the TV and gets his coat.

'About time,' says Catherine, as she goes to open the door. 'Right. The rat was last seen over there.' She jabs her finger in the direction of an antique Welsh dresser that dominates the far end the kitchen. You need to catch it, put down poison or traps or whatever, clear up and get out in half an hour as I've got some very important guests coming and I cannot have... oh god, this is so vile.' Catherine goes to put her hand on Selwyn's back to propel him into the room but then thinks better of it and instead ushers him in with a flap of her hand. 'We'll be in the drawing room. Just let yourself out when you've finished.'

Selwyn takes a long breath in through his nose. He holds his hands out in front of him, gently patting the air as if it was a solid mass. With eyes closed he stands absolutely still then, imperceptibly at first, rocks back and forth, faster and faster, like a worshiper at the Wailing Wall. Exhaling sharply he opens his eyes, flexes his fingers, and walks slowly towards the dresser.

It is a female rat, about eighteen months old. No teats are visible on her belly, suggesting that her latest brood are now capable of fending for themselves. Selwyn pictures them below the floorboards, heads cocked, hearing the final squeal of their mother. He holds her aloft by her pink, sparsely haired tail and considers her glossy coat, off-white teeth and bulbous eyes, which now stare vacantly at the floor. He can't help but admire the creature. Teeth that can gnaw through concrete; whiskers so sensitive that they can detect the slightest change in direction of the finest breeze; an incredibly acute sense of smell; the ability to dig, jump and swim, even underwater; a gut that is as happy processing cardboard as chocolate – their favourite food – and intelligent to boot. Shame they have to be killed really. Should be killed, at any rate.

Behind the dresser is a hole between the skirting board and the polished oak floorboards. It is just big enough for a rat, albeit a small one, to squeeze through. Selwyn reaches for his coat and takes out the remaining finger of the Kit Kat and his newly sharpened knife. It doesn't take long to make the hole a bit bigger. He puts the Kit Kat next to the hole. Then, placing his hand flat on the rat's limp back, he begins to cut.

>><<

A large, black chauffeur-driven car draws up just as Selwyn leaves. His stomach rumbles as the smell of the casserole follows him out of the door. He hopes he'll pass a shop soon so that he can sate his chocolate craving. A bit of Green & Black's should do the trick.

By the time Catherine's very important guests are seated Selwyn is back home. As Jonathan eagerly tucks into his smoked trout pate, Selwyn is making himself a cup of tea. Just as the thought that the venison is a bit gristly crosses Donald's mind, Selwyn decides the time is right to break open his bar of chocolate; and at precisely the same moment that the sugar and cocoa alchemy causes a sigh of contentment to escape Selwyn's lips, Jonathan's ghastly wife opens her mouth wide as she lifts her fork from her plate, the rat's tail wound between the tines.

LEWISHAM

Pro Creation

Pro Creation

Andrea Pisac

'Cunnilingus was a very familiar manifestation in classical times; ... it tends to be especially prevalent at all periods of high civilization.'

Havelock Ellis, 1905 (British sexologist and social reformer)

Olga had heard that Goldsmiths College, especially the art department, was one of the most innovative and progressive in the country. She would have considered it as a way to do something different with her life even if she and her husband hadn't lived five minutes' bus drive away. Actually, that summer, when she went to speak to one of the tutors about the possibility of studying there, she noticed that most people cycled into the College. If accepted, she decided, she wouldn't take the bus again. Instead, she would ask Steve to help her choose a bike – not a fancy one, but something that would fit in with the Goldsmiths crowd.

Factually speaking, Olga and Steve had a happy, monogamous marriage. There were some disclaimers, as with all partnerships: *you can do this, if I can do that; I will turn a blind eye to this if you ignore that,* type of thing. There was also the one of a quite serious nature that was not about fitting around each other's annoying habits. They believed that if they allowed themselves as much freedom as possible, a licence to grow their own little world separate from each other, they would forestall adultery and safe-proof their marriage forever. In reality, this meant they could fantasise about whoever they wanted to, socialise with whoever they wanted to, even exchange bodily warmth with other people if they were that much attracted to them. The only thing they couldn't do was engage in penetrative sex outside their bond. Though the agreement was verbal, drawn up quite spontaneously one night early into their marriage, it had worked for them for over ten years.

After Olga and Steve left Croatia and moved to London, she had a sense that Steve had been getting more out of their agreement than her. It was why she decided to take up studying art. The marriage was still solid, Olga was certain, but things had changed from how it was in the beginning. Back then, Steve would get upset about not being able to understand the conversations she had with her compatriots. Especially text messages and emails that made her giggle, reminding him that she had always been a tiny bit of a stranger to him. When she spoke on the phone in Croatian, particularly late at night, Steve would come up with something that needed to be addressed there and then; or he would start playing with her hair, shoving his ear close to the phone to hear if the voice was male or female. Olga was also certain that he went through her birthday cards. And though he couldn't understand what they said, it was quite possible that, over the years, he noticed the one with the same handwriting that ended with the word *ljubav* – *love* in Croatian. That much Steve did understand. That and the fact that *ljubav* in Croatian was rarely used to describe sentiments between friends.

If she was guilty of anything it was of holding on to a few ghosts from the past. She herself paid little attention to them. But Steve's reaction to having her little world made her want to nurture it and grow it bigger. It gave her the upper hand in the marriage. Holding back just a little bit, while her conscience was clear, she thought was a good way to keep Steve on his toes. Then one Sunday morning, as they went out to have breakfast in their favourite café in Greenwich, she discovered he had a little world of his own too. It was more real than hers.

Steve was an investigative journalist. In Croatia his speciality was exposing dishonest politicians. Back in London, he switched to pursuing slimy drug dealers, people traffickers and pimps. He claimed that the change was necessary so they could have a more comfortable life. Tabloids paid better and they needed the money for their mortgage. Olga felt for Steve. She saw his spirits crushed every time his piece was published in the *Sun* or *Sunday Mirror*: no credit, his writing massacred by editors, framed with pictures of half-naked women in distress. Every Sunday Steve drank more than usual and she kept her mouth shut because she felt for him. Neither did she complain about her having to work in a bookshop because her psychology degree was not recognised in this country.

That particular Sunday, as they were sipping their coffee, Steve proudly opened a copy of the *Sun* on the page with his story. His job was to expose a prostitute who was conning people by continually selling exclusive rights to her virginity. The project had gone very well, Olga could conclude from looking at Steve's glowing face. It was a full page article in a prominent place in the paper, accompanied by a photo of a young woman sprawled naked on a hotel bed. The writing was dumbed down, as usual, but Steve was less bothered than before. He actually snatched the paper away from Olga's hands before she could finish reading it. The piece had brought them £1,500 and it was a reason for celebration. He suggested buying wine and chilling out in the park and at that point, Olga knew that he had stopped drinking to fend off depression – he was enjoying his depraved adventures. They had a big fight that afternoon with no resolution. Olga wanted what he couldn't give. Because the pleasure he got from investigating prostitutes was Steve's little world.

Olga and Steve never talked about that afterwards. More articles and field trips followed, all involving naked, victimised women. The way Steve wrote about them, and the way he made love to her afterwards, were proof to Olga that those were titillating experiences for him. Still she chose to believe that her husband never broke their verbal agreement. Instead of asking and finding out, Olga made a new plan to introduce equilibrium between their worlds: hers had to become much more important and pleasure giving.

Olga's old portfolio of drawings wasn't enough to get her into an MA in Fine Art. She wasn't ready to give up studying at Goldsmiths, not after Steve offered to pay for her fees, so she went for MA in Art and Psychotherapy. She hoped the course might help her feel she was good enough to be an artist. Maybe being close to those lucky ones who actually practiced art would inspire her. Their youth, their unwavering faith in their work, their hair styles and skinny jeans – she quickly fell in love with all of that and she wanted a piece of it for herself. At coffee breaks, she joined their debates about reducing carbon footprints, overturning global political conspiracies and installing the social state. Those free spirits challenged the world as she knew it and they soon became part of her own world. It was more than just academic; they shared a real emotional bond, especially her and Jamie – a quiet visual artist from the crowd. Everything was going according to her plan: she was receiving enough pleasure at the College so, in the evening, when Steve came back from work, he would find her relaxed and smug in her armchair. Her little world was no fantasy any more.

By late October, she was eating lunch with Jamie every day. Olga never felt awkward about it – Jamie was a misfit himself; in his late thirties and the only one in the group who took up Fine Arts to find a new meaning in his life. For the rest of the people, the course was a logical step on from their well-established, though short, careers. The first strange moment between Olga and Jamie happened as they walked out to the back lawn to have lunch and enjoy the last days of sunshine. She looked at the red ivy leaves covering the back façade of the main building and said how beautiful they were. Jamie first looked at the leaves, then down into his trainers, smiled and looked into her eyes. Later he will keep reminding her that it was then he totally fell for her.

Most evenings the crowd went to Rosemary Branch – a pub at the far end of the College on the road leading to Lewisham – to avoid other students who frequented the popular Goldsmiths Tavern. Rosemary Branch marked the border between the College and the rest of Lewisham. But from the outside, it was difficult to tell because departments on that side occupied a row of Victorian houses. This non-institutiaonal look of the College property was why the pub was claimed by both local drinkers and art students. The dark and shabby looking space came alive as young artists drank beer and discussed must-see exhibitions. Olga and Jamie often 'forgot' to rejoin the table. They would stay at the bar, fighting for space with local men who watched football on the big screen. Olga had taken up smoking again – it was actually after the 'virginity on sale' article that she broke her ten year sobriety from tobacco. She didn't overdo it, only two or three rollies, for which she would take an eternity to fold and lick together. Keeping her focus on the tobacco paper between her fingers felt safer than having to look at Jamie all the time. He told her she should not smoke; not in a patronising way, but with an honest assertion that 'she must know she was stronger than her impulse to run away from feeling what she needed to feel'. What she felt was a strange kind of elation from being next to Jamie. And even though she thought of him as un-pretty, with a small scrawny body, she was drawn to him. It occurred to her that doing art, after so many years of not drawing and painting had an almost religious effect, the kind that inclines one to see beauty in everything and everyone.

Early on it was established that both Jamie and Olga were in committed relationships; Olga had Steve, Jamie had Clare. It was easy for both of them to talk about intimate details: there was nothing at stake. So, Jamie told Olga that he and Clare had very limited sex, that she had trouble receiving pleasure and that as a logical consequence the frequency of their love-making had dropped significantly in the last five years. Jamie used his film editing skills to put together online porno film tasters. He played the footage to himself when he was at home alone. Olga was the only one who knew about it, but instead of making a big deal about it, she made silly jokes. It was easy, she wasn't the one being lied to and dumped over porno stars. When Jamie was in a really good mood, she knew she could call him a wanker and that he would laugh really hard keeping his gaze fixed on her lips.

Olga felt that her marriage had become much better since she started spending time with Jamie. There was less tension, she stayed and ate out at least three times a week and she rarely asked Steve when she should expect him home. Life became mellow, as if corrected with film editing software. In the morning, Olga now rarely worried about how Steve was handling phone conversations with his editor and if he had someone to help him. She could easily focus on her studies and art assignments. And when she stayed at home for the day, she made sure she was never hungry at the same time as Steve, so she could sneak out to the park and eat her sandwich while on the phone with Jamie. The last time Steve asked her to help him with translating something, she turned him down. When he brought a female translator to the house to have tea before taking off to the field, she knew his worries about her little world were growing, as expected.

Steve never nagged. The only way Olga could sense his slight worry was through his actions. Inviting his brother, plus wife and children, over for dinner was one of them. Helping out with grocery shopping and cooking spoke even louder. Steve talking about sex while they were chopping vegetables came almost as a shock. First, he apologised he hadn't been very sexual recently while Olga kept her knife on onions. Then he held her from behind and before kissing her ear, he whispered what he had planned for them that night after their guest had gone. Her favourite thing – that's what he would do, and that's how scared he was. Olga didn't get her hopes up because her favourite thing was Steve's least favourite thing. She did feel excited enough with the prospect of any old sex. Predictably, though, Steve's brother provoked him into a long, conflicting political jabber that dragged far into the night and had to be smoothed over with large quantities of wine. By the time the guests had gone home and Olga put the plates into the dishwasher, Steve was barely awake enough to ask her for a rain check.

By the beginning of the spring term, Olga and Jamie had disclosed various details of each other's sex lives. They usually did it in a pub, sitting close enough to the rest of the crowd to avoid any suspicion, and far away enough to keep the conversation to themselves. Laughing away their issues over a few rounds of gin and tonic made their faces flush. With each giggle they swayed towards each other, sometimes touching one another on the shoulder with their foreheads, only to retreat back to the same position on a bar stool – like a pendulum. But when Jamie teased out Olga's biggest sexual issue that needed addressing, they both remained upright, staring at each other. She stated in a matter-of-factly, almost medical, way that she had not received cunnilingus in the last three years and that her frustration was reaching boiling point. Did he think she was spoilt for expecting married sex to keep being as fulfilling as it was in the early days?

Olga was not sure what exactly went on between Jamie and her. He seemed to be able to fill every vacancy that Steve left by retreating to his little world. Whatever she complained of as missing in her life, Jamie volunteered to quench it. And they weren't small things, or things at all – they were feelings. She wanted to be told she was beautiful, he wanted to tell a woman she was beautiful. His girlfriend could never receive a compliment. She wanted to be listened to, he wanted to listen to a woman.

Because his girlfriend talked for a living and just wanted to be silent at home. She wanted to receive intense oral pleasure, he was desperate to give it to a woman. His girlfriend was the love of his life but she could not enjoy sex. Olga wanted to keep both her marriage and her little sexual world and Jamie promised he would never do anything to jeopardise that. After all, he could never leave the love of his life. Not after being together their whole adulthood so far, and certainly not after buying a house together. So what was it that the two of them had?

Jamie claimed it was all to do with art. For the sake of art, they had to push themselves over the boundaries they had created. No one could be a great artist without forsaking the limitations of labelling things, people and experiences, he said, quoting one of his teachers. Olga, awe-stricken by the Fine Arts department where she was not accepted, thought that made perfect sense.

The end of the spring term party coincided with Jamie's girlfriend going away to a conference. It was the last time the crowd would have drinks together because the summer term meant no lectures and all creative practice. After several rounds and sitting at their favourite spot at the bar, Jamie dared Olga to ask him to give her cunnilingus. This was not a joke any more, he explained to her. She had to deal with expressing her desires and being able to receive what she requested for. So Olga did. In the car, on their way to his house, she phoned Steve to tell him she was too drunk and was staying over at a friend's house. And when she ended the conversation, she made another request of Jamie – there would be no penetration. He smiled in the way of approval, his eyes never leaving the busy road through Brixton. That made Olga's little world grow bigger than it had ever been without violating her marriage agreement. She was breaking the limitations, while staying within the limit. The feeling of sweet weightlessness in her chest spread through her arms and down to her lap. She rolled down the window and thrust her head out to breathe an unusually warm spring air. Maybe she was ready to become an artist, she thought.

In the summer term, Olga and Jamie did their creative practice outside the College. The beneficial effect of artists creating in a group was not in their interest any more. They had found another way of catalysing the raw energy of inspiration, and of walking through boundaries to find new perspectives. After the first night of oral stimulation that made Olga climax so intensely that she couldn't calm the twitch in her thigh muscles for hours, their joint project continued with more frequency and pleasure. Now they did it either in her house or his when their respective partners were out. Matrimonial beds in both houses were off limits, so they kept to the sofa, carpeted floor, or the shower. The only guilt Olga felt was to do with thinking that there was nothing in it for Jamie. She was the one who received all the time, received with the rich vocal outpouring of satisfaction. And though he managed to convince her that giving her pleasure and seeing her convulse in the paroxysms of her sexual bliss was what he was after, he eventually admitted he did want something else – for her to scratch and smack his bare arse.

At home with Steve, Olga felt slightly worried. For the first time she wasn't fretting about his little world growing – new seedy articles or scantily clad language assistants who were invited over for tea. It was the total lack of her interest in what he was doing, who he was developing feelings for, who he was fantasising about while masturbating that made her brood. The frequency of their love-making had been in the range of once in three to four weeks, and she hardly missed it at all, let alone complained to him. They had grown enough apart that the marriage disclaimer of *no penetration* now seemed to have been taken out of the context, uprooted from the emotional ground that it was supposed to protect. Why not go all the way, Olga wondered? What was the purpose of keeping within this limit? That said, for Olga, breaking away from the marriage was never in the back of her mind. She loved Steve.

In July, Steve announced that he had to go on a six-week field trip to the Ukraine. Olga was genuinely sad. She held him for a long time in front of the departures sign at Heathrow Airport. And on the way back, while sitting on a Piccadilly line train, she felt lonely, as if Steve's trip reminded her of having lost something much earlier in the year. Crossing the boundaries is always connected with leaving the old ground behind, she remembered Jamie telling her. So a few hours later, when she came back to the house and tidied away Steve's breakfast dishes, she felt much better. The unsettling eeriness was gone as she remembered that everything in the next six weeks would be about creative practice – right there at her home.

During one weekend, when Jamie was able to stay the night as his girlfriend was out of town, they touched on a new topic. Over a lavish meal they couldn't even finish, Jamie asked Olga if she thought they had been cheating on their partners. Were they having an affair, he asked her. Olga was not entirely sure if Jamie was troubled by the pangs of guilt or his artistic commitment was slacking, but she knew this – he gave her the best cunnilingus and she wasn't ready to give that up. Art or no art. So she told him it was unproductive to define their practice as an affair: that would limit their work and their artistic growth. What they had, she convinced him, required no labels and so wasn't a threat to their respective relationships. Jamie showed no relief after that. His face twisted in a slight yet very distinct sort of pain – a pain of a lover being rejected. He told Olga he was developing deep emotions for her, something that was superior to the commitment he felt for Clare. To Olga, Jamie suddenly felt like a fraud. If he was just using her to deal with his own emotional rubbish, it wasn't fair. Even so, she stopped herself from throwing a tantrum – while a succession of blissful sexual scenes flooded her mind – and decided to play along. Developing feelings was normal, she soothed him. But no, they were not committing adultery and they did not know where all this would lead them. It was painful for her to come so close to breaking her marriage disclaimer, but that night, she let Jamie enter her with his finger.

During the six summer weeks Olga and Jamie's breaking of boundaries stayed within the agreed limit. They slept on the sofa mattress, which was permanently arranged on the living room floor. What they had going defied any labels. It was certainly not an affair and not a secret relationship. They were not in love with each other so there was no need for them to ever feel guilty of committing adultery. If anything, they felt proud that they had been influencing each other to grow as people, which surely was only a bonus for their respective partners. Their creative practice reached unprecedented heights. Jamie felt delirious with his arse being smacked until red raw. The sessions were initially administered by Olga's hand but later included other objects obtained from sex shops. His emotional release was often followed by short but intense bursts of tears – which was great for his art, he told Olga. The finger concession, on the other hand, that Olga reluctantly and fearfully agreed on, turned out to be more than a valuable experience. Olga had her first G-spot orgasm. She wouldn't even know what it was had she not read somewhere that there were three different types of female orgasm.

At the end of August, Olga submitted a much-praised dissertation on using art to develop a freer sense of sexual self. Jamie's work was a two channel installation: a close-up of his bare arse being spanked by a leather whip set to a loop on one screen while on the other he read definitions of random concepts from a dictionary. After they submitted their work, they had coffee on the back lawn and watched the leaves that still hadn't turned red. Steve was back home, the course was over and it was time to slow things down. At least that's what Olga suggested. She walked Jamie to a back street behind Rosemary Branch and hugged him by his car. When he drove off, she walked back home. The traffic was so thick, she was faster than 21 bus which kept crawling by her side.

***

It was several weeks before Steve agreed to a difficult conversation with Olga. This time she nagged. There was no logic in keeping hold of their overgrown little worlds any more. The distance between them didn't make her want him more as it had done in the past. Before the words were uttered, she knew they had both lost the battle. Steve confessed going all the way with prostitutes he was reporting on. It was a combination of things, as he explained to her. One was certainly her growing coldness in the months before his trip. Olga looked at his defeated face. Then she slapped him really hard. He stood motionless, waiting for more. It was strange but for a moment it all seemed like another annoying thing spouses do to each other, something that could blow over in a few days. But then she realised that it was Steve who had crossed the line they had agreed on – not her – and that was mostly why she was so angry. Because she wanted to forgive him, but it was not up to her. Their agreement wouldn't let her.

Olga and Steve said nothing for a week. They slept in the same bed and went on with their days as usual. In the evenings, they both decided to spend time with each other. They cooked together and then watched TV while holding hands. One morning, while Steve was at work, Olga met up with Jamie. They drove south for an hour, parked in a quiet, leafy spot and had penetrative sex. It was good. Jamie was gentle, he could make it last long and all the while he kept whispering into her ear that he loved her. While Olga was buttoning up her blouse, he told her he really meant it. It wasn't only a sex routine and it had nothing to do with art, he said in a more determined tone of voice. He was leaving his girlfriend. On the way back, Olga said nothing, she only cried. Jamie kept one hand on the wheel and the other on her knee. He glanced at her from time to time while repeating in a slow monotonous rhythm: everything will be fine, we love each other.

***

Some lines cannot be crossed, Olga repeated in her head in the weeks ahead. Steve said it after confessing his indiscretion. But perhaps if both people crossed the same line, they could make a new agreement, with new lines. She slept with Jamie to give them a chance at a clean slate. The idea almost made sense, so they kept talking about their future. In reality, they spent more time crying behind each other's back. And then, just before the beginning of winter, they separated. Olga knew that if they were ever to divorce, they wouldn't remain friends. He would always be her Steve, and she could never stop wanting him.

A year later, though, Steve insisted on attending Olga's graduation party. It made her happy. They drank champagne on the back lawn, standing awkwardly far from each other. It was a sunny day and she sweated underneath her gown and cap. The leaves were red again. She could barely see Jamie at the opposite end of the lawn, holding hands with his new girlfriend. When their eyes met, she pretended not to recognise him.

GREENWICH

Notes to Support Funding Application Modestly Proposed to the Woolwich Tourist Board

Notes to Support Funding Application Modestly Proposed to the Woolwich Tourist Board

Stella Duffy

Dear Sirs,

Please see below outline for a promenade performance, to be conducted over five afternoons/early evenings, in and around Woolwich Town Centre in the London Borough of Greenwich during summer 2011, leading to a fortnight of events during the 2012 Olympics, Woolwich being perfectly sited to welcome visitors from Stratford.

We propose that this piece will more than adequately cater for the many tourists (primarily but not exclusively from North America and Western Europe) who regularly flock to visit Woolwich's famous sites over the summer months, and will also encourage them to visit the lesser known attractions – e.g., Eltham Palace, Greenwich Park, the Maritime Museum, Observatory etc. We further predict that even locations north of the river (Canary Wharf, the Isle of Dogs) could benefit from some of the spillover. It seems only fair that a centre of such world-renown as Woolwich should make more of a conscious effort to share some of its gains with the less-lauded areas of the Borough, and we look forward to making this possible through our work.

We await your response with interest,
Two Sisters Arts

The Characters

Sister 1: is a nurse. She has just finished night shift at the Dagenham Ford factory. She is the mother of four adult children with three grandchildren. One of these adult children died fourteen years ago – orphan and widow/er are useful terms, there is no word in English for the parent of a dead child. She has had three hours sleep and prepares for the journey to Woolwich. Transport for London has predicted it will take her an hour.
(For promenade purposes, we envisage a bus journey from Essex into SE18, the reverse of the journey undertaken by so many working class families when they 'migrated' to Essex in the 60s and 70s.)

Sister 2: is a maker. Books, cakes, theatre, gardens. She lives in Lambeth. TFL predicts her journey – two overland trains via London Bridge – will also take an hour.
(We imagine the possibility, with TFL's assistance, of collecting groups of audiences at both Denmark Hill and London Bridge. We are also in talks with the Thames Clipper service about the potential of an integrated journey downriver from Westminster or Waterloo Piers, to Greenwich. Again, this would bring our promenaders past the lesser known elements of Greenwich – Cutty Sark, Observatory, the Painted Hall – on their way to the more popular tourist destination of Woolwich Market.)

The Journey

Once on their trains the Sisters (and their collected audience members) begin texting each other in an on-the-move multi-media flash event. Starting at two different destinations in a journey forward to their past.

The Show

On arrival in Woolwich, the Sisters perform the classic 'Which Exit Are You At?' sketch, so beloved of our audiences who have seen us work up the same routine very successfully at Oxford Circus and Waterloo Stations, and also across all levels of the Barbican and the National Theatre.
(If time and funding allow there is a possibility this could be extended to include a Woolwich Arsenal/Arsenal–Islington stations comedy mix-up, similar to the company's highly successful 2008 show: 'Oh, I Thought You Meant The Other Lyric – Lyric Hammersmith/Lyric Shaftesbury Avenue')

Having met and united their Essex and south London audiences, the Sisters will then begin the actual **Woolwich Promenade**. Based on the original journeys taken by those working 'up town' in the 1960s, the Sisters will walk from the station to the Ogilby Street flats and back again, taking in sites of particular interest in the journey. These include (but will not necessarily be limited to):

Woolwich Market

Sister 1 tells Sister 2 about the time she became lost in the market. She was only separated from her mother for a moment, but was 'found' by a kindly local woman who whisked her away to the Police Station before the mother had a chance to find her child. She was later retrieved from the Police Station by an irate and relieved father. Sister 1 recounts that even at a young age she was aware that the father was torn between the two options of tears of relief or rage at the child for getting lost. She recalls being surprised not to be hit for getting lost and noting that the father was expressing a conflict of emotions – something she had not previously seen in him.
(For educational purposes, we believe this will provide a very useful opportunity for teacher & school groups to discuss the changing nature of behaviour towards

children, not least in the use of corporal punishment. Appropriate material will be included in our Schools Pack.)

Woolwich Library

Sister 1 marvels that not only are the carved wooden banisters of her childhood still intact, but the large wooden doors are still very much part of the main building and must obviously be used when the building is fully locked. The sisters then discuss, in Dr Seuss-like rhyme and rhythm, the first books they read, or that were read to them, in a library. They share the feeling that the Children's Library always seems warmer and more comfortable than the adults' section, and how – as children – they used to sneak adult books from the shelves and sit reading in quiet corners. They did not do this in the same library, but in libraries almost 12,000 miles apart. The action however, was the same – a librarian reads to a group of small children, that group of small children discover that stories can also happen outside the home, the world is never quite so small again. E.g.:

The books that we found in the corners of town
The books that were there on the carved wooden stair
The books and the stories their glorious glories
They took us to places and found us new spaces and they were quite aces
The books we found there.
The books that were tales of drama and whales,
and wails with an I, and Wales with no aitch, or whales with a Y
(there's a Y in your wayles? Like fayre and like tayles, the olden days spayles ...)
Spells.
The library smells. That peculiar, junior, scents of a room for you,
Place for us, space for us, here on the shelves for us.
That's what we found in the library in town.

(Our intention is to include local children's lines in creating an epic poem/story with potential for our promenading audience to join in on the choral line, 'that's what we found in the library in town'.)

Mulgrave Primary School

At the site of Mulgrave Primary School, now the Mulgrave Early Years Centre, both Sisters share with our audience the games of their childhood. On the school playground (permission has been sought), the audience are divided into teams and play games of hopscotch, kick-ball, four square, keepy-uppy, tag, hide and seek, stuck in the mud (aka candlesticks), culminating in an audience-wide game of British Bulldog. After the games the audience will be further entertained, as they catch their breath, by the local children's choir. In case of bad weather (though this is exceedingly rare in Woolwich's excellent micro-climate) the games will be moved inside to include drafts, chess, Monopoly, Twister, Operation, the Game of Life etc.
(The games will give a chance for our audience to enjoy each others' company, create intra-audience relationships, and also to relive their own past glories. We are proud to say we believe this makes us the first UK theatre company to fully comply with the new government-approved Arts & Olympic Council ruling UK-A&OCE106789.5 that it is not appropriate for any member of an audience to remain in a static position for more than one hour at a time, all shows therefore to have an element of participative physicality. We expect to include children from all parts of the borough in the choir.)

Walk To Ogilby Street

The walk, via John Wilson Street and several smaller streets, into Frances Street to see the shops of note (including the newsagent's where Sisters 1 and 2 went every Saturday morning to collect 'the books and papers'

– *The Magic Roundabout* comic, *Bunty, Tammy,* and *The Woman's Weekly*), will bring in street entertainment in the form of parkour-trained poets performing acrobatic leaps from billboard hoardings, utilising the street-running form to turn the billboard frames and the Arsenal's old brick walls to sites of performance poetry. This technique was first pioneered in 1967 by Sister 1, under the auspices of Big Brother, and has also been noted by Sister 2 in the London Boroughs of Lambeth and Wandsworth. We believe that by extending the parkour form to include active poetry we can enhance what is otherwise simply a physical activity, adding a literary and emotive element.

(We are also aware of the sadly under-used walls and hoardings in neighbouring Greenwich, most especially those alongside the Observatory and Greenwich Park. We trust that our use here, in Woolwich, will encourage Greenwich residents to see the multi-function possibilities of their own walls, thereby giving them hope that their own area might one day achieve some of the international recognition, usually only given to Woolwich and, on occasion, Eltham South.)

At The Flat

Stopping at the council block, childhood home of Two Sisters Arts (also of Big Brother, and the original Four Older Sisters Company), Sister 1 and Sister 2 will lead the audience in a Climb Up the Stairs, a chance to enjoy the startling Original Blue of the wall tiles. On the first landing we will offer Tales From The Shute – a series of inter-connected pieces about rubbish recycling, drawing on stories from all twelve families living in the block. On the top floor we will engage in another participatory programme, this time encouraging the oldest members of the audience to climb on to a recreation of Sister 2's original 1967 tricycle, and – as Sister 2 did in the 1960s – race against themselves in timed trials the length of the balcony that connects all three top floor flats.

(We perceive this intergenerational work to be one of the highlights of the season.)

Sisters 1 and 2 will also recreate the famous 'Up the Slope' image from 1967 – attached.

We will then recreate, in Flat 8, two parties that occurred in 1967. The first is the infamous Parents' Night Out Party. Sisters 1 and 2 having been left in the care of Big Brother and the Four Older Sisters Company. There was a large and diverse 'youth' party, mostly young people aged between 15 and 21, with music from a number of popular bands of the time, several friends of friends, and various trips with little girls (in nighties, dressing gowns and slippers) to the off-license. Whereas in the original, this was halted at an early time and involved numerous young men climbing three floors from the balcony down to the ground, then running off into the night accompanied by the shouted threats of Angry Father and Worried

Mother, we propose that Party 1 will segue smoothly into Party 2 – The Farewell Party, in which Family of Four (comprised of Sisters 1 & 2 and The Parents) prepare to leave for New Zealand. Music for this will be a medley of Mrs Mills' Party Favourites and Irish Pub Songs on a looped track, while we will offer our audience the classic south London party delicacies of sausage rolls, and sliced egg and bacon pie.
(The first of these parties will use members of the local Youth Theatre, playing an earlier generation version of themselves, thereby again fulfilling the requirements of our intergenerational funding application. The second will provide ample opportunities for school groups to engage in a sociological study of the white working class in late 1960s Britain and their attitudes to their own emigration, while geography students will no doubt benefit from studying the route of the Family of Four's subsequent journey on the Shaw Saville Southern Cross – taking in Trinidad and Tobago, the Panama Canal and several of the Polynesian Islands.)

Lead-up to the Finale

This section of the promenade will feature a firework display on Woolwich Common, using – as is appropriate for the location – live ammunition. It will be supervised by those of the MoD currently stationed there, and will use the toddlers from the Woolwich Common Nursery School to create a tableau displaying Woolwich's history from its Iron Age beginnings, through the founding of the dockyard, the establishment of the Military Academy, the incorporation with London, and finally the opening of the UK's first branch of McDonald's in the town centre. The walk back downhill will take in various art deco delights and will allow the recreation of another landmark moment, that of Sister 1's regular flight from the back of an old Routemaster at the roundabout between the two deco cinemas. This fare-dodging tactic was well known in the late 1960s and will be recreated here by a team of acrobats on board an original Routemaster bus, brought out of retirement for this purpose.

The Finale

The audience and all performers will by now have re-grouped outside Woolwich Town Hall, the doors will then open and, as if they are rising from the black and white tiled floor, an assemblage of market stall holders, all dressed in black and white, will erupt from the Town Hall. They will lead the audience through to the market where, with a medley of traditional British songs, and very much in the style of Stanley Holloway in *My Fair Lady,* they will begin a simple routine of dances designed to allow the public to join in. When the audience are sufficiently engaged, the music and the routine will then change to the now theatrically obligatory (but nonetheless enjoyable for that) Bollywood form. The black and white attire of the market holders will turn inside out to reveal a multitude of colours.

We expect that by now, with public and performers engaged together, there will be upwards of 500+ people, dancing, singing and enjoying learning the simple routines together in a dance route that takes in Woolwich Market and the waterfront.

At the waterfront, the Sisters will again divide the group into two : Sister 1 will lead the first group underneath the river via the Woolwich Foot Tunnel, while Sister 2 takes the second group over the river on the Woolwich Car Ferry.

When all audience and performers have assembled on the north side of the Thames, the Thames Barrier will be raised and lowered, synchronised in time with the pulsing Bollywood beat.

Then, from the southern shore, the assembled audience will see the Green Man rise above Oxleas Wood, walking downhill to the township of Woolwich. Sited comfortably beside the Woolwich Leisure Centre, the Green Man will then beckon the people back from the less-popular north to the glorious south.

(Operated by cranes, and held together by a simple yet effective pulley system, the

Green Man is actually made of 504 metre-long canoes which, when laid end-to-end, span the width of the Thames at this point.)

The Green Man comes to the edge of the water, his powerful and enticing voice now clear above the music, and lays himself down across the water, so that our audience and performers can walk back across the Thames, on a bridge made of his linked, upturned canoes.

When all have crossed safely, the Green Man will reassemble for a moment before sinking beneath the river.

(All the canoes are attached to miniature buoys and will be retrievable the following morning.)

One last chorus as one remaining rocket lights the sky, then there is a final glimpse of the Green Man beneath the water, and the show is over.

Sisters 1 and 2 will lead the audience back to the centre where they will enjoy a pie and mash supper (vegetarian options available) before boarding their respective forms of transport and heading home.

Predicted outcomes :

- increased interest in the areas surrounding the thriving centre of Woolwich, such as Greenwich, Blackheath, Shooters Hill – areas that usually do not benefit from Woolwich's high recognition factor among tourists/theatre-goers which will also enjoy the knock-on effect of those audience members who choose to stay overnight and look around the next day.

- through showing the better-known history of Woolwich it is envisioned that audiences will become more interested in the history of the whole area, and may even be persuaded to visit the Greenwich Museums, Eltham Palace etc.

Final statement

We, of Two Sisters Arts, are committed to sharing our vision, and to bringing the prosperity and privilege enjoyed by the lucky denizens of Woolwich to all. As children allowed to roam free across Woolwich Common, through bomb sites, and derelict Arsenal buildings, we know 'our' Woolwich offers a truer insight into the heart of London, than for many of those for whom home is a 1930s semi, an Edwardian mansion block apartment, or modern river-view penthouse. If successful in this grant application we pledge, not only to endeavour to share this good fortune within the wider reaches of the borough itself, but also to reach still further in future. We hope to share Woolwich's privilege with those eking out a living in the Royal Borough of Kensington and Chelsea, the many suffering in Islington, and maybe even to those languishing in the outer reaches of Richmond upon Thames.

We aim high, and with your help, Woolwich Tourist Board, we can do it.

Two Sisters Arts, March 2010

BEXLEY
The Sugar House

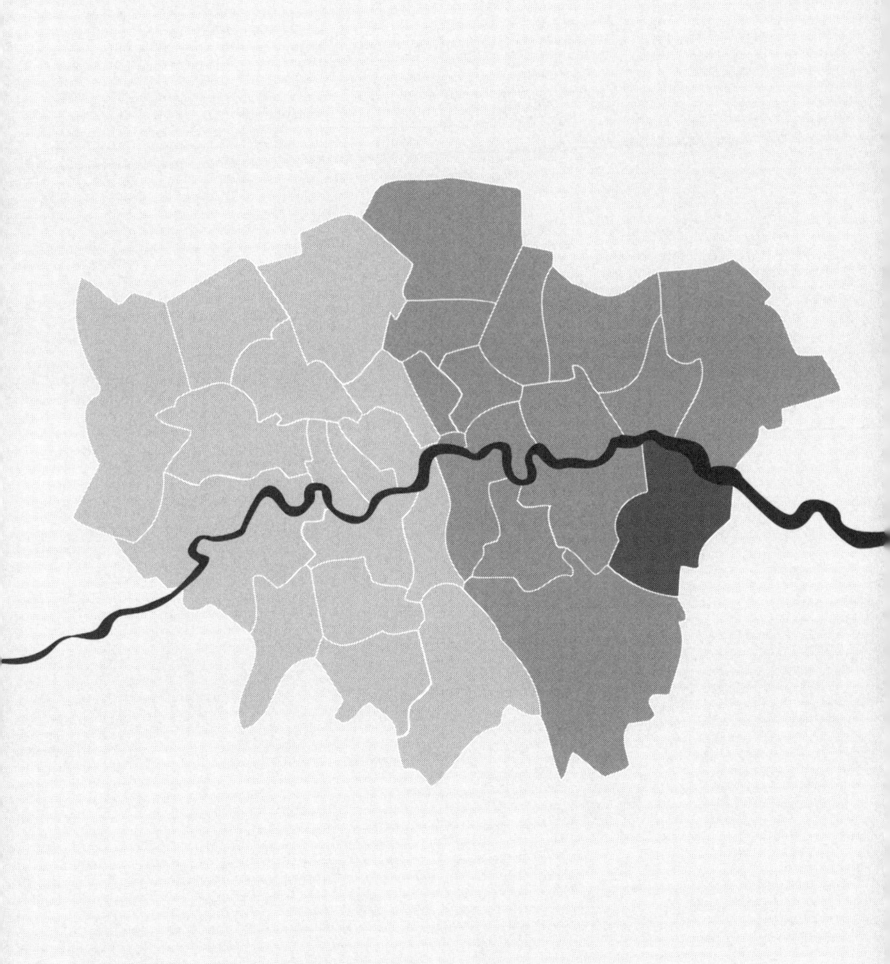

The Sugar House

Emma Darwin

Up in the elm tree the breeze catches my frock so that it flaps and flitters like a sooty flag, black muslin for Grandpapa Bean. In the sun my bow's curly gold and the flights on the arrows are dark and fierce. I'm standing on the first thick branch and though there are few people about yet, I can hear everything... the clip and shush of the grooms as they take round the early morning feed, the clank of the scullery pump, the crooning pigeons and even the hoot of the first up train on Grandpapa's railway over the hill at Abbey Wood.

When Nannie took me to see him, I knew he was dead but for a moment I thought he'd turn his head and smile, the way he always did when we went in to say our Collect on Sundays. And then we got closer and I saw that he wasn't there: that he'd gone. 'To Jesus,' said Nannie; 'To God,' said Grandmama; 'Earth to earth, ashes to ashes, dust to dust,' *said Mama, reading the Funeral Service to us all in the nursery, and crying the whole way through. Who will look after his railway now? I couldn't help wondering. Who will make sure the rails are safe and the viaducts strong as the trains pound to and fro, full of girls like me and mothers and fathers, housemaids, soldiers, milk and chickens, parcels of silk and crates of china, letters from London and hops from Kent?*

Beyond the house the lawns are split by the blue of the lake, and the far side is a smudge of trees, some still winter-dark and others bright and new. I sling my bow over my shoulder again, and tuck the quiver into my sash. Then I climb higher, crook by crook, bark smooth under my hands, until I'm among the leaves.

Driving through the park we glimpsed the house. Natasha's only comment before we were past the gap in the trees was that it *looked* like a wedding cake, and how on earth was Grandpa Barber going to get up all those steps in his wheelchair? Always supposing he was still well enough to come.

Big, dark, specimen trees and close-clipped hedges lined the road again. 'There'll be a lift somewhere,' I said, giving her knee a friendly rub before I had to change down to turn into the car park. 'Everywhere's accessible these days.' She said nothing, just shifted her knee out of range. 'We only need have a quick look round.'

'They'll give us the hard sell, Alex. Even party venues must be finding things tough.'

'Okay, let's pay to go round just like any tourist. Then if we think it's a goer we can ask to speak to the events manager. It's got to be better than upstairs at the Crown & Greyhound.'

We left the car in the still empty car park with my cameras locked in the boot and walked back along the road, which was too narrow to have a proper pavement. A catering supplies truck passed us, close and fast over the speed bump, and Natasha flinched. 'It'll be much more expensive.'

'Well, if it's too much we'll do something else,' I said soothingly. On the gravel sweep before the house a notice said that Danson House opened at ten. My watch said ten to.

'So now what do we do?' said Natasha. 'Don't forget I've got to be at the Refugee Council by one.'

'And I've got to be at the studio at two. Shall we look round outside? We might be able to see the garden. If the weather's like today–'

'Yeah, right, in August. As if.'

'There'd be plenty of inside if it isn't.' She didn't answer. 'Look, we can get round that way.' I started to walk towards the trees to the left of the house, and she followed me. 'It looks so imposing, but it's not actually at all big, is it.'

No, not big at all for a what you'd call a great house, but as perfect as something drawn by a talented child, and a precocious one too; it wasn't a flight of fancy, not a gingerbread cottage or castle with towers like medieval hats, but a vision of the plainest, purest shapes: cubes, rectangles, triangles, half-hexagons. The classical forms, the golden mean, a building not earthy or even earthly, but spun from mathematics. And as we stood and looked at it, the sun came round and swept the dirty yellow-grey of early morning from every face, leaving each a pale, different gold.

'If it *is* a wedding cake, then they haven't put the white icing on yet,' I said, one eye on Natasha. 'It's still marzipan.'

She smiled, reluctantly perhaps, but then she reached up and pulled down my head to kiss me. We stayed like that for a while, and I thought how good she smelled in the cool warmth of the April sun: shampoo and toothpaste and her favourite scent, and under it all something so female... She rubbed her cheek across mine, and my heart turned over. 'I love it when you've just shaved,' she said. 'It's the only thing wrong with morning sex, but now...'

'Mmm...' I said, kissing her again. Her cheek was always softer against mine than I remembered. And so was her body, I thought. She pulled a little away from me, smiling, then snuggled back. 'And morning sex, is, of course, Alexander Oyenusi, absolutely the *only* reason you offered me house room...'

'It's a fair cop, Miss,' I said vaguely into that specially sweet bit under the corner of her jaw. After so many months of us taking it in turns to shuttle to and fro between London and Liverpool, for a whole month while she did this course I could go to sleep with her, I could wake up with her, reach for her, find her... and still every morning, every day, she was sweeter and more delicious than my memory could hold on to. I rested my chin on the top of her head. 'Can we be like this forever?'

She went rigid, then suddenly there was a yard of cold space between us. 'Not you as well? Don't tell me you're thinking about weddings too!'

'Don't be daft, Tash,' I said, taken aback. 'Who said anything about weddings? It's just a party for my Grandpa and Grandma, which I said I'd help with, and you said you would too.'

'Yeah, okay,' she said. 'Look, they're opening. Did you say there's a café? I need some coffee, and then let's get it over with.'

Higher and higher and towards the light. There are more people down on the ground now, going about their business. There are two I don't know; I settle myself astride a branch and look down properly. The lady looks cross, and the gentleman looks like a picture in the magazine that Grandmama reads about the African missions and all the people they help. When I was little and didn't like my dinner, Nannie used to tell me not to be so fussy because I was lucky to have any when so many people were starving in Africa. Once I asked why I couldn't send the toast crusts and rice pudding and sardines off to them in a parcel with plenty of stamps. I half expected a scolding, but she just laughed.

The lady and gentleman are holding hands as if they're getting married. But you can marry someone, and they die anyway, maybe not long after; they die, and leave you behind. Is it worse when you've only just learnt to love someone, or when you've loved them almost all your life? Is it worse to be the one dying, or the one left behind? Grandmama says she'll be joining Grandpapa soon, that he's happy in Heaven and she will be too. But she cries nonetheless, as if she doesn't quite believe it.

The café, the booklet said, was once the breakfast room of the house, and it had old photographs on the walls. Collodion prints by the local photographer, by the look of them: the gamekeeper outside his Gothick thatched cottage; a be-skirted little boy glaring uneasily at the camera; three young ladies dressed for a coming-out ball; an elderly gentleman reading a book to a pinafored girl of about twelve.

There were french windows out onto the lawns but they weren't open. 'It's a bit chilly still,' the lady who brought us the coffee said. 'Are you here for long? We might be opening them for lunchtime.'

'I'm not sure,' I said, feeling Natasha shift uneasily beside me. 'It's a lovely house, though.'

The waitress settled her tray on her hip. 'Yes, it is, now it's being looked after properly, after all the vandalism. Of course the grounds have changed. The elm disease was bad hereabouts – they lost a lot of trees. But inside... lucky they had all sorts of stuff – these photographs from the Bean family, and the Boyd things even older. Brings it alive, doesn't it. Sometimes you can imagine the family's only just stepped out for a breath of air... And where are you from?'

'Biggin Hill,' I said, and of course she said, 'I mean, where are you *really* from?'

'Biggin Hill.' I said again. 'Kentish born and bred.'

'Oh, I see,' she said, and after a moment. 'I'll just get your croissants.'

As she trotted off Natasha smiled at me and murmured, 'Shall I tell her about my Russian grandfather? Just to confuse things?'

'So which of your family can come?' I asked, pulling out my phone. 'Have you heard yet?' There was a text waiting. 'Oh good, Great-uncle Frank says yes.'

'I don't know. I haven't asked. It's bad enough having Granny with that look in her eye.'

'What look?' I asked, clicking on the list of my grandfather's family. 'Barber, Francis, hm, where are you?'

'The *isn't it about time you and Alex got married* look, of course... Mum even asked once! Asked, straight out! Alex, are you listening to me?'

'Yes,' I said, and did.

'Then will you please stop going on about the bloody guest list?'

I put my phone away. 'Sorry.'

The waitress returned with our croissants.

In the grand entrance hall the sun had barely had a chance to warm the stone or bring the marble busts to life, but the steward was keen to explain things. 'John Boyd inherited a business importing and exporting sugar,' he said. 'It was *the* great industry of the eighteenth century, the way to make fortunes as railways were in the nineteenth. And he also owned a fort in West Africa, exporting slaves to work the sugar plantations in the West Indies.'

No flicker at what he'd just said, but then he'd be used to talking to school trips. But Natasha said, 'Ouch!' and turned away to make for the first of the main rooms. I thanked him and followed, and saw her glance quickly away from the congregation of little gilt chairs and start to study the paintings. Plump, un-alarming Classical deities, all pearly satin robes and significant gestures, fitted nicely between the grand mirrors. Cupids climbed vines between the windows, a muse played a flute, and Bacchus was a pleasant young gentleman carrying a jug. Plenty of natural light, if I were scouting a job, but they already had a souvenir guide and postcards. It faced east and a bit of south from the bay, so it might be a bit gloomy for the early evening drinks that we were planning.

'Not much sign of where the money came from here, though,' Natasha went on. 'More Versailles than St Vincent. But then there never is, is there? Perish the thought that they should be reminded of the bones under their feet.'

'I know.'

Another steward with a thick folder strolled puposefully towards us. 'It's lovely, isn't it. This is originally the dining room, but when we host weddings the ceremony takes place in here, though the rest of the house is yours too: you take possession for the day. Were you thinking of holding an event?'

Natasha turned and walked away to the next room so abruptly that the lady looked worried.

'We are thinking of an event, but not a wedding,' I said quickly. 'An anniversary party.'

'Oh, how lovely. Is it your – your – parents?' she asked, more cautiously.

'No, my grandparents. It's their Diamond wedding anniversary.'

'Diamond! Goodness me, how wonderful! You don't hear of that very often these days. Did they meet in the war?'

'Yes, my grandmother was in the American army. Hers was the first African-American women's unit to go overseas, and my grandfather was in the RAF. They met in France.'

'What a lovely story,' she said. 'Usually it's the other way round. I mean, the GIs and so on.'

I grinned at her. 'I don't think she was overpaid, though she brought her own nylons with her. And my dad's from West Africa, so things sort of came full circle.'

Natasha had come back. 'Alex's American grandma can tell you stories about slavery,' she said loudly. 'She heard them from *her* grandfather. He was born a slave.'

'Goodness,' the lady said again. 'I do hope she'll write it all down some day. It's such a shame when these memories don't get handed on.'

Higher and higher again, into the thick of the leaves. The branches are thinner here; they move in my hands and under my feet, and everything rustles and shifts about me, almost as if the tree itself is breathing. I can't see the ground so well now for all the leaves. If I were Robin Hood and wanted to shoot a deer, I'd have to aim carefully. I used to practise and practise so I could be part of Robin Hood's band. And then Grandpapa gave me the storybook, and I was sitting in the library window because the lamps weren't lit yet... And when I got to the end of the book it felt like the end of the world – everything – Robin Hood was dead – how could anything be left? Someone came in. Everyone was kind, but it was Grandpapa who really understood.

Sometimes I used to dream I had wings. Not silly baby wings, like the Cupid and Psyche above the library fireplace, but like the angels in my Sunday picture book: long, fierce wings with thick feathers, so that they could fly down from Heaven and sing Gloria in excelsis Deo. *Nannie says that people become angels when they die, but I don't think Miss Barber believes that, because she had a very up-to-date education at a university before she became our governess. Or are they like faeries? The sort she was telling us about when we were reading* A Midsummer Night's Dream? *Living for hundreds of years, then withering away like a leaf in winter because they have no souls. Dust to dust, grey dust like a ghost, blowing away in a puff of wind.*

Will Grandpapa come back as a ghost? I don't think I'd mind if he did. I think I'd rather that, than know he's gone forever.

Not bones under our feet but the kitchen, still being restored but the steps down to it health-and-safety approved for visitors. A wide, black range set into the wall, pots and pans, knives and pudding basins, and gadgets, all black iron and worn wood, for slicing hams and carving loaf sugar. Small, thick arches hinted at cellars, and light was funnelled down from windows high in the vaulted ceiling, to slide like bright water over the copper of the saucepans and lie in stretchy patches on the stone floor. The light flickered and I looked up. The windows above our heads were at ground level for the people going about their business outside; the flicker was their passing shadows.

There wasn't much more to see, but I felt reluctant to climb back up the kitchen stairs. Up there was the pleasure palace – the show house – a confection of cream and gilt. But down here was solid brick and wood, Windsor chairs, work and food and a fire. Even in the wash of morning light I could imagine it in winter, at night, with the range lit and glowing, lamplight licking into the corners and vaults, the sweet, drunken scent of rising bread, and the crackle of dripping in the pan.

'I suppose we could even have the party *here*,' I said. 'It would be nice and original. We could carry Grandpa's chair down between us, me and a couple of the men. Though from the light point of view the library would be the best room – it faces west. Mind you, that little chamber organ – how mad is that to have in your house? It does make it rather like a church. Handy for weddings, I suppose.'

Natasha turned on her heel, ran up the stairs and disappeared through the door at the top.

I caught up with her outside on the gravel as she stormed towards the road. 'Tash, what's the matter?' I said, though I knew what the matter was.

'Did my mother put you up to this? Are you softening me up? Waiting till it's all warm and lovely at the party, and everyone's thinking the same thing. *Wouldn't it make Grandpa and Grandma happy before they finally go – at Grandpa's age it might be tomorrow. Joining the families – wouldn't it be romantic?* And all that sort of crap, and I'll be full of champagne and you'll ask, and I'll feel all the family pushing me to say *Yes*! Mum and Granny most of all!'

At least now I knew exactly what she was so angry about, but how dared she think I'd go behind her back like that? 'Your mother hasn't said anything of the sort! If she wants you to have – to have what she was denied... She's never talked about it, and if she did, I wouldn't insult you by joining in. As for the party, I'll be far too busy making it happen. Have you any idea how peculiar my family is? And yours isn't much better, you said so yourself. Full-time management job.'

'You don't have to invite my family.'

'Yes I do – how could we leave them out?' Too late, I realised that, *they're how we met*, was hanging in the air like the worst kind of rom com, the one which ends with confetti in the sky.

She was standing very straight, counsel for the prosecution. 'So you expect me to believe that my staying with you – organising this party – none of it's a test?'

'A *test*? Dear God, Tash! Why would I want to test you? I love you, and you make me happy. I – I thought I made you happy too.' I held out a hand, as if to bridge the gap between us but without much hope, and she didn't respond. 'I love you, and I want to be with you. That's all.'

The breeze suddenly whisked through the air between us, brushing my cheek and swirling her hair. It seemed to start a smile inside her that spread to her mouth and eyes, and they were still smiling as we wrapped ourselves together.

'I love you too... ' she said happily, and then ages later, 'Are you serious about using the kitchen for the party?'

'No. I think we should be as grand as we want. All that gilding, all those gods... Let's take possession of it, for Grandma and Grandpa.'

Up here, I can still believe in flying. I used to think Grandpapa would live forever, but he didn't, and when I'm back on the earth I'll know it. In a moment I'll climb down and look for that arrow, but not just yet – not for a moment – not till the sun moves on.

BROMLEY

The Penge Missives

The Penge Missives

Emile West

Thursday, 7 January 2010

Dear Eleanor,

I spent a good couple of months pondering how I would open this letter. I googled, I asked friends, I even went to the Maple Road library to consult books on etiquette and decorum. Alas there is no tome entitled *How to Say 'Hello' to a Loved One a Decade Later*.

A decade later.

I find myself at a loss to understand how ten years have passed so quickly. And what has been gained and lost. After much thought and consultation I came to the conclusion that the best three words to open this letter would indeed be:

I am sorry.

I can clearly see the rise in your eyebrows, your beautiful blonde arches casting a shadow on this very page. But this is the truth. And it has to count for something. And I can't think of three better words to write to you, and so I begin.

You may be wondering how I found you. Serendipitous perhaps, but I ran into Dan at Beckenham Road Station. Now don't be angry with him, he put up a good fight, but I managed to squeeze him for your address. I expect he gave it up because he thought I'd be too sheepish to contact you. This was in December. He was there with Jackson, who's grown into a fine young man (though he didn't remember me). We tried to make chitchat, ended up sitting in different sections when the train arrived. I'm surprised that you've moved north of the river. I never thought that would happen.

I'm still in the two-bed in Penge. Few things have changed. I redecorated the bathroom, the boiler passed. One winter I considered getting a cat, sharing it with the mismatched couple next door. You can forego calls to the RSPCA, it didn't happen. Henry Porter plus Cat – a recipe for disaster, I know. The biggest change, and in many ways the spur to my contacting you, has been that after nearly twenty years of loyal service, I have been sent to pastures new. The last time I remember scenes like this was in '91 when that unfortunate chappie met a rough tide on his yacht. I was 35 then, in my prime you could say, and I weathered that storm quite well. This time it was like a giant black veil descended from the ceiling, enveloping the picture desk. Deathly silence, not even the rapping of keyboards or curt telephone calls.

The actual conversation was a blur. I drifted off and found you as my anchor. We were back in Florence, must have been spring '98, taking a walk after dinner, pausing as we crossed the Arno. Yes, it's the moment I asked you to marry me. And you said 'Yes' almost like you were asking a question. I needed that memory then. The pursuant regrets barbed me. I knew that I had to make amends. Regrets are like children, the more you give them thought the more they grow and beget yet more and more regrets. In this respect, you could say I am a grandfather.

I went home early that day, caught the train from Victoria, got off two stops late and bought a packet of cigarettes. I toyed with the cellophane, considered how my finances would be stretched, eventually threw the packet away much to the delight of a passing teenager. A week later I cleared my desk.

So that's that. I'll stop writing now. I hope you'll forgive this letter and understand that I'm trying to figure quite a few things out. I shan't ask you for anything, but I will write again soon.

Yours,
Henry

Wednesday, 10 February 2010

Dear Eleanor,
I hope this letter finds you well. I am in better spirits than the last time I wrote to you. Seems rather funny to be writing letters again. There has to be some space left for the written word without facsimile. Well, this should be with you soon enough, if the postal workers don't keep going on strike.

You may wonder why I am writing to you again, considering you haven't replied to my first letter. The truth is I found solace in the process. I hope you don't think it selfish of me to write again. There's no fool like an old fool. First time I ever thought of myself as old. In some respects I'm nearing maturity. I'm sure that would make you smile.

I spent most of today in a grotty office near Kings Cross. As part of my settlement, I now have a counsellor and a career coach. The career coach is sombre at best. I think persistent contact with the newly unemployed has killed his spirits. He slouched as he read my curriculum vitae, then practiced a few interview questions with me. I asked him if we could swap roles, so that I could be the interviewer. He straightened up then, not quite getting the joke because the joke was him. Time up. I went and sat in the waiting room. It was rather like a doctor's surgery, fleeting eye contact, terrible magazines, general malaise.

I went to see the counsellor, who asked me how I felt. She sat opposite me, and with a quiet voice said that I should try new things and spend at least thirty minutes exercising each day. For some reason I told her about the letter I wrote to you. She nodded appreciatively then – and here I don't know why – I told her about how I left you at Down House. I guess you never found out that I drove back and looked for you. You must have caught the bus. Seems rather silly for a relationship to stumble over the theory of evolution. But it really was the beginning of the end. It's one of those things in a relationship, like which football team you support or which newspaper you prefer to read on a Sunday. When you told me that you had a relationship with God, well I didn't quite know what to do. And it's in those situations where we fare the worst.

Suffice it to say, the counsellor was at a loss for words.

I went back to Penge and paced along the High Street. I stopped at a Jamaican cafe and had jerk chicken, black beans and rice. I was the only white man in the establishment, though I didn't feel unwelcome. I sweated and emerged to the February gloom not quite sure how I would finish the day, which leads me back to you. I'm caught in two minds as to the purpose of retrieving the past. The Americans call it closure. But I'm not wanting to close things up, quite the opposite really.

I'll stop there Eleanor.

Yours,
Henry

Tuesday, 23 March 2010

Dear Eleanor,

I take it you sent me the pamphlet on Creationism. Very funny. I actually read it from start to finish. My point of view remains unchanged. If you can post me this, why can't you write me a short letter, just a few lines about how you've been? I asked my counsellor if I am stalking you. She answered by asking me if I had applied for any jobs. I think her and the career coach have swapped places.

My news is that I've taken to walking around Crystal Palace. Being *sans emploi* I have gained weight, seems like those twice-daily games of sardines were actually good for something. I walk around the park anti-clockwise, so past the athletics stadium, a brief pause by the dinosaur lake, past the maze and then take a seat by the beheaded statue (poor chap). I make my exit by the bus terminal.

The creak in my knees sounds like a gate in need of oil, and as this blasted winter drags on I'd rather stay in bed, but it has helped me discover a brave new world. It's funny to see that there is another eco-system of people moving about between the hours of nine to five. Mothers with their prams and growing expectations, young men most likely up to no good, old people, so many old people, and then the unemployed. It's rather like being in limbo – so many souls caught in the fog-filled park.

I've made a new friend, a spritely septuagenarian called Gerald. The first few times I saw him we would nod politely and say 'Good morning', then we reached the point where we were either going to ignore each other completely, or start a conversation. Not one to waste any time, Gerald asked me if I was out of work. I filled him in, he mashed his false teeth and shook his head. He's a retired publisher, quite a fascinating fellow really, he used to publish poetry. So he's either brave or mad. We talk briefly each time we cross paths. I don't know how long it will be until I invite him round to the flat for tea.

Perhaps I'd be better placed if I said I met a delightful woman in the park. I haven't. I couldn't make it up if I tried. In the past ten years there have been three women in my life, none of them of much consequence. I'm not trying to flatter you in saying that they weren't a patch on you. Back in December I asked Dan if you were married. He didn't want to answer, was probably contemplating lying to protect you. It was actually Jackson who said that you weren't. Kids can't help telling the truth. So here we are in our fifties, single, footloose and fancy free. Surely it's worth a try?

I may be holding myself as a hostage to fortune, but I expect you are thinking about the baptism. I was hoping I could apologise without having to mention it. I am sorry. It really was a silly thing to do. Remember that I was there doing it for you, so we could marry. And the priest did say that I wasn't the first to come dressed as Elvis.

You see my difficulty with faith is that those who possess it have a tendency to believe that those who don't are faithless. Life is never so simple or reductive. Yet instead of intelligent conversation, I resorted to farce. And I lost you.

Yours,
Henry

Wednesday, 25 May 2010

Dear Eleanor,
Funny how life seems to fold in on itself. Nearly forty years ago I set out from Sydenham to start as a junior at a local newspaper in Wapping; now I have returned to a much bigger newspaper, albeit in a much reduced capacity. I've been given a three-month contract to work on the picture desk, not in print, just for their website. I cannot begrudge it.

This huge, devouring city continues to amaze me. I commute on the new East London line, a brief walk to Penge West then twenty minutes to Wapping. Myself and many of my fellow passengers board with a sense of delight and wonder. New places previously forgotten have appeared on the map, even the school kids are happy to sit on the orange and brown seats. In this post-Industrial age, it still is possible to get people excited about trains.

For a picture researcher it's ironic to say I could do the job with my eyes closed. I try not to let my mind wander too much though. After work I sometimes walk to St Katharine Docks, and ride up to Shoreditch. I feel like a much younger man up there. A drink in one of the grungy bars. And then back to Penge to the two-bed flat *sans chat*. To watch television, eat and sleep.

I have tried Eleanor. I must say that these letters have helped me through a difficult time. And perhaps it has been for the best that you haven't replied. Even men like myself hold romantic notions about the one that got away. All that remains to say is that I am here, and you are there, and one day we might meet in the middle.

Yours,
Henry

Index of Contributors

ANDREA PISAC

Andrea Pisac was born in Croatia, 1975. Her 2001 collection of short stories *Absence* won the award for the best debut book from the Croatian Student Union. In 2007 her second book *Until Death Do Us Part or I Kill You First* was published. She is currently working on a novel, for which she has received a mentoring award from Exiled Writers Ink in London.

strangerstoourselves.blogspot.com

ANGELA CLERKIN

Angela Clerkin is a writer and performer. Her screenplay *Head Over Heels* is currently under option and she has two plays in development. Angela also regularly freelances for *The Green* and *Westside* magazines. TV appearances include: *Holby City, EastEnders, Sugar Rush, My Family, Dalziel & Pascoe* and *The Office*. Angela was born and raised in north London.

ARIANA MOUYIARIS

Ariana Mouyiaris is a born and bred New Yorker who has lived in five countries and traveled to countless others in search of the perfect neighborhood to hang her hat. Hopefully hybrid and constantly searching for imaginative narratives, she is always looking for an excuse to keep her camera snapping and a cabbie to tell her how things have changed.

ASHLEIGH LEZARD

Ashleigh Lezard's writing experience ranges from covering economic development for the Financial Time Group to penning a monthly column on the trials and tribulations of living as an ex-pat in Hanoi. She has lived in London on and off for ten years.

BOBBY NAYYAR

Bobby Nayyar was born in Handsworth, Birmingham in 1979. He was published in the anthology *Mango Shake* (Tindal Street, 2006) as well as in journals and magazines. He's been based in London since 2005 first in north London, now east. In October 2009 he founded Glasshouse Books.

theyearofpublishingdangerously.co.uk

CHARLOTTE JUDET

Charlotte Judet studied Psychology at university then spent 10 years working for small publishing houses, where she edited illustrated non-fiction books. Now she combines attempts to write fiction with freelance editing and looking after her two young daughters.

DEBORAH O'CONNOR

Born and bred in the North-East of England, Deborah O'Connor now lives in east London. She read English at Newnham College, Cambridge and last year produced the BAFTA-award winning poetry documentary 'Off By Heart' for BBC2. She is currently at work on her first novel.

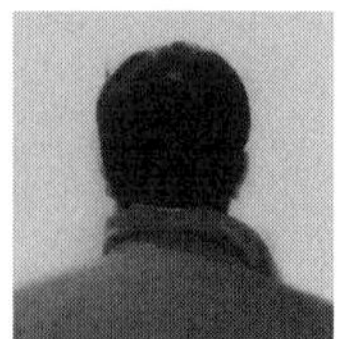

EMILE WEST

Emile West has lived in and around London for over six years. He is an aspiring playwright and poet.

EMMA DARWIN

Emma Darwin is a London-born novelist who was brought up in Manhattan and Brussels before settling in Southwark. Her debut *The Mathematics of Love* was shortlisted for, among others, the Commonwealth Writers Best First Book. Her second novel, *A Secret Alchemy*, reimagines the world of the princes in the Tower; her third is in the works.

emmadarwin.com

KADIJA SESAY

Kadija Sesay is the founder of SABLE LitMag, editor of several anthologies and series editor for Inscribe, (a Peepal Tree Press imprint). Her poetry, short stories and essays have appeared in anthologies and journals in the UK, US and Africa and have been broadcast on BBC World Service.

MARTIN MACHADO

Martin Machado is a lecturer and a transition coach, helping people to achieve their full potential. He was vice-chair of the Hackney Chamber of Commerce and a founding member of the East London Chamber of Commerce. He lives in east London with his wife and two young sons.

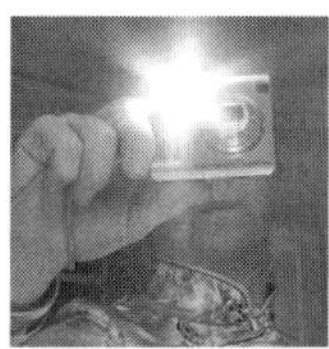

RICKY OH

Ricky Oh isn't his real name. Writing isn't his day job. London isn't where he was born. He doesn't keep dogs. He is not size 8. He is no longer in his thirties. He is not very good at DIY. He doesn't ever tell lies.

www.3fishinatree.com

STELLA DUFFY

Stella Duffy has written twelve novels, forty short stories, and eight plays. Her latest novel, *Theodora,* is published by Virago. She was born in Woolwich, lived in New Zealand from the age of five to twentythree, and now lives in Loughborough Junction, Lambeth.

stelladuffy.wordpress.com

SUSANNAH RICKARDS

Susannah Rickards lived in east London for fifteen years but now lives south of the river. Her debut collection of short stories won the Scott Prize and will be published by Salt in October this year.

TABITHA POTTS

Tabitha Potts was brought up and attended two schools in east London before going on to Oxford University where she gained a First in English Language and Literature. She lives with her family in Tower Hamlets, where she also runs a business, Mimimyne.

www. tabithapotts.com

UCHENNA IZUNDU

Uchenna Izundu is an energy journalist; her short stories have been published in *IC3: Penguin Book of New Black Writing in Britain*; *Tell Tales:* Vol I; *the anthology of short stories*; *Fathers & Daughters: an anthology of exploration,* and *Sable Litmag*. Her work has also been broadcast on BBC World Service.

About Glasshouse Books

Glasshouse books has a simple mission statement:

To publish books for people who don't read.

Certainly this is open to interpretation. To clarify it means we're trying to reach people who can read, but choose not to read books, be it because they don't have the time, or they don't know what to read, or we're simply not publishing books to cater to their tastes.

Each of our titles focusses on a different area of the market, from helping young people make their first steps into professional life, to celebrating the richness and diversity of london. Uniquely we commission every title we publish.

As part of our remit to reach more readers, we make versions of our titles available to read exclusively on our website:

glasshousebooks.co.uk

In 2010 we will be publishing 5 titles, each one beautifully designed, printed to respect the environment and featuring many exciting debuts.

Books for *me, you, everyone.*

Our titles: *100, Boys & Girls, Bloody Vampires, 33 East* and *33 West*

People

GLASSHOUSE BOOKS

LONDON metropolitan university

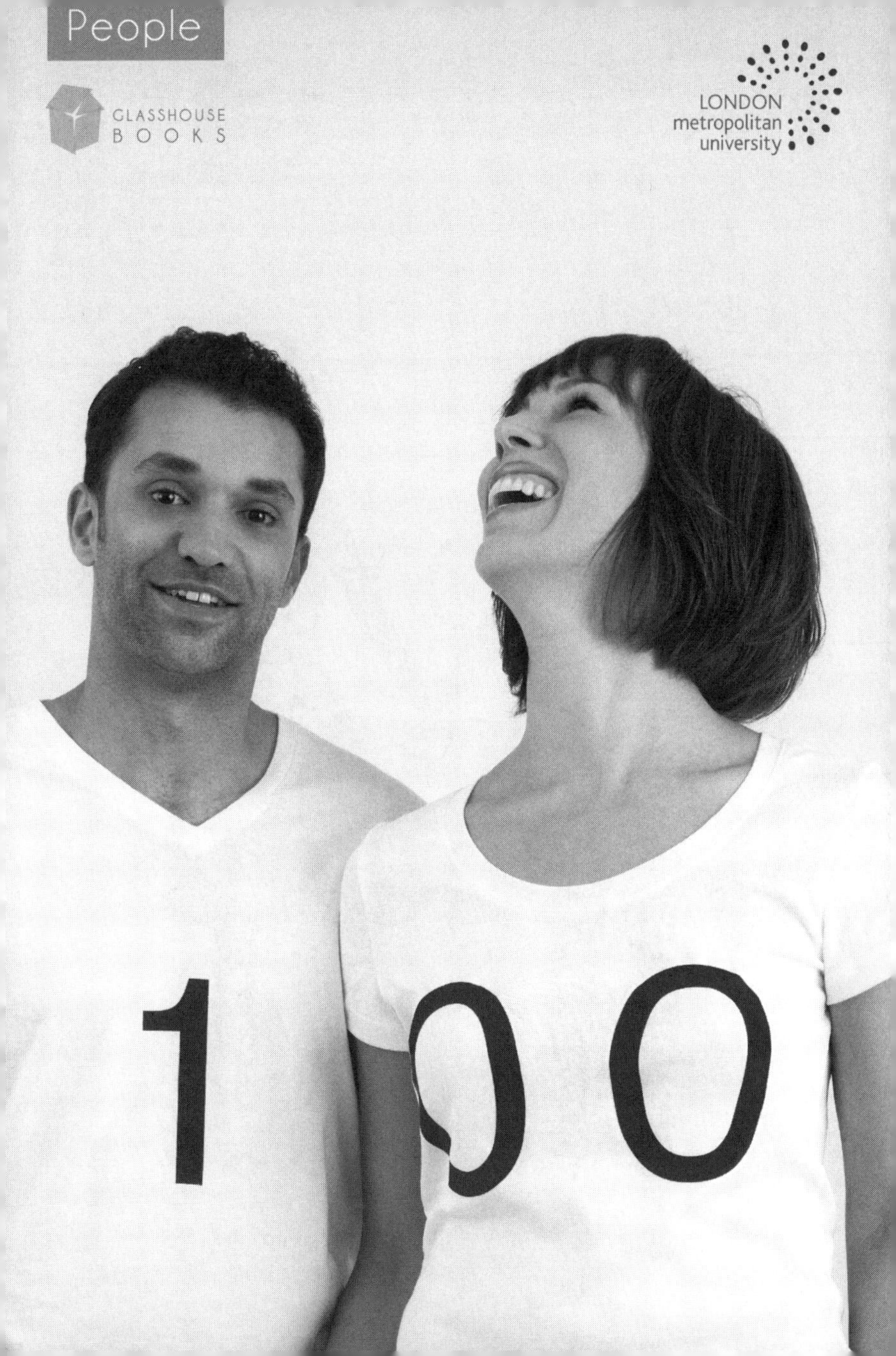

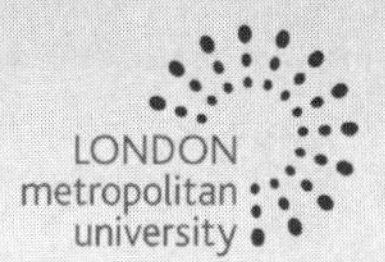

Shorts

GLASSHOUSE BOOKS

THE ALBERT KENNEDY TRUST

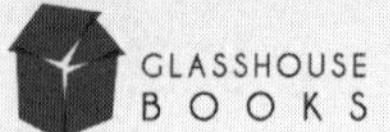

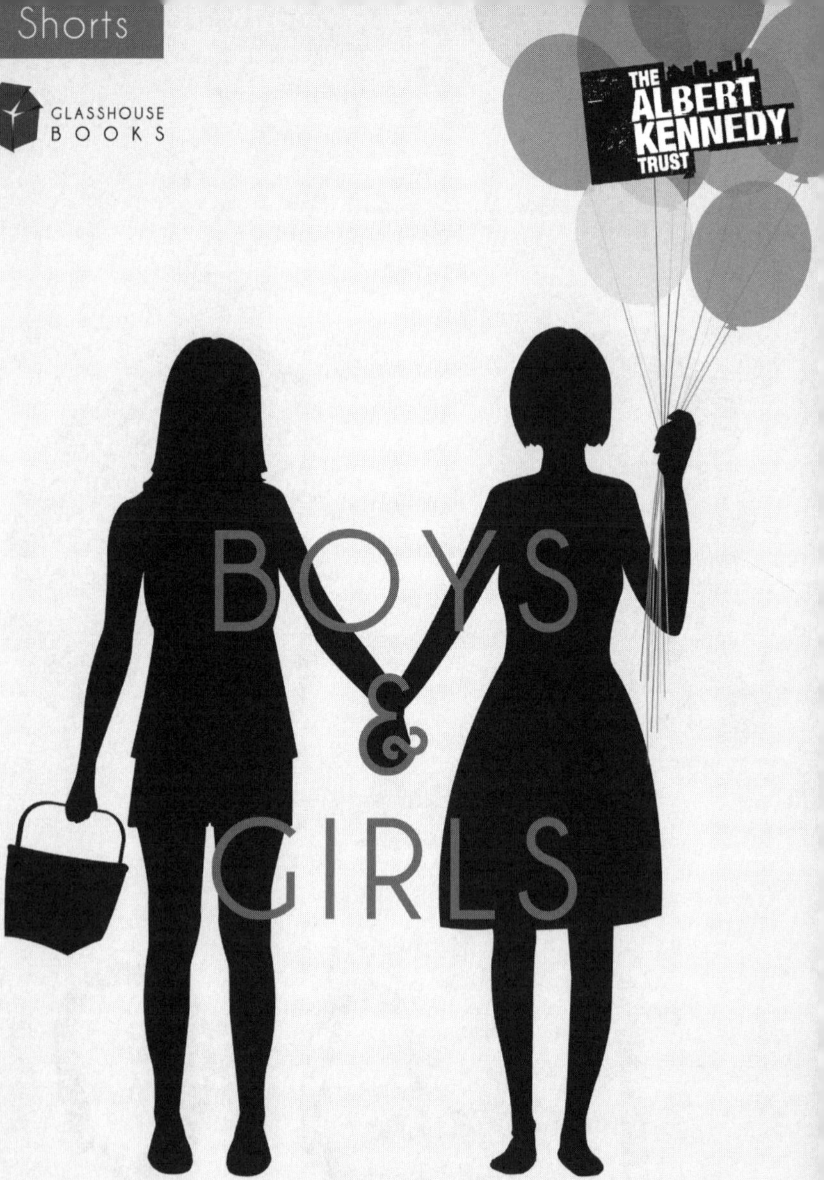

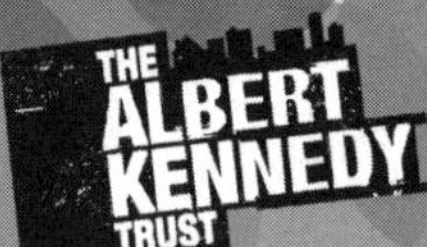

BOYS & GIRLS

Edited by Paul Burston

Shorts

A Glasshouse Books Collaboration

Design by Eren Butler

Edited by Bobby Nayyar and Charlotte Judet

Assisted by Kate Du Vivier

Typeset in Arno Pro & Champagne & Limousines

First published 14. 07. 2010

ISBN 978-1-907536-33-5

Glasshouse Books
58 Glasshouse Fields
Flat 30, London
E1W 3AB

glasshousebooks.co.uk

facebook.com/GlasshouseBooks

Printed and bound in Great Britain by TJ International Ltd, Padstow, Cornwall

How to order

Please email sales@glasshousebooks.co.uk or call 020 7001 1177. Alternatively, you can buy online at glasshousebooks.co.uk.

For trade enquiries please contact Turnaround on 020 8829 3000 or email orders@turnaround-uk.com

100

£10
9781907536007

Bloody Vampires

£10
9781907536663

33

£15
IN 2 VOLUMES

BOYS & GIRLS

£10
9781907536090

Me. You. Everyone.

glasshousebooks.co.uk